one year commencing

one year commencing

Kathy Stinson

Thistledown Press Ltd.

Canadian Cataloguing in Publication Data

Stinson, Kathy
One year commencing
ISBN 1-895449-65-0

I. Title.

PS8587.T56054 1997   C813'.54   C97-920046-6
PR9199.3.S75054 1997

Book design by A.M. Forrie
Cover art by K. Gwen Frank
Set in 11 pt. New Baskerville
by Thistledown Press Ltd.

Printed and bound in Canada by
Veilleux Impression à Demande
Boucherville, Quebec

Thistledown Press Ltd.
633 Main Street
Saskatoon, Saskatchewan
S7H 0J8

Saskatchewan
Arts Board

THE CANADA COUNCIL | LE CONSEIL DES ARTS
FOR THE ARTS | DU CANADA
SINCE 1957 | DEPUIS 1957

We acknowledge the support of the Canada Council for the Arts for our
publishing program. Thistledown Press also gratefully acknowledges the
continued support of the Saskatchewan Arts Board.

Dedicated to Paul's daughter
wherever she may be

one year commencing

july

one

will not need this, I will not barf. Al tucked the airsick-bag between her knees. The grey and red pattern of the plane seat in front of her jiggled and swam. She refused to look out at the shrinking prairie quilt. Usually she loved the force of the plane hurtling forward, pushing her back against her seat, the sudden light emptiness as the wheels lost contact with the runway. But not this time.

For a crazy instant Al pictured herself running up to the cockpit. *Wait, go back. There's been a mistake.* But the tattered paper she'd read so many times she knew it word for word — a copy of the only important page of the court order — was tucked in the pocket of her denim jacket. And maybe it was a mistake, but it was also real. Decided years ago by some stupid judge who didn't even know her. Didn't know how well she got on with her mom, who was probably in the old Toyota on the road home now with a wad of wet kleenex on the empty seat beside her. Didn't know about Sam, who said she'd wave from her yard when the plane flew over, "but it won't be *good-bye*," she'd said, "just *see you.*" Didn't know about her other friends either, who threw the going-away party for her last week. They all rode out on their bikes together after pizza, to share her last experience of a prairie sunset. It was spectacular, too — the purples, pinks, and oranges growing deeper and deeper over the rise of land by the river, and the fields that went on forever, under a sky that did, too. Until gradually the dark swallowed it all up. Stupid judge didn't know anything.

"Headphones?" the flight attendant offered.

"Thanks." Al shoved the airsick-bag back into the seat-pocket. A good movie, any movie, would take her mind somewhere else.

Except *Mrs. Doubtfire*. She couldn't laugh today at anybody's divorced parents, no matter how funny they were supposed to be. She yanked the plug from the arm of her seat and leaned her forehead against the cool window.

Below her sprawled big rectangular farmers' fields, sliced in pieces by long straight concession roads. They were neat, orderly, the way her life was — up till now. Living in Alberta with her mom and spending a couple of weeks of summer in Toronto with her dad. She saw him for a few days around Christmas, too, when he came west to visit his parents. Things were fine just the way they were.

Until this summer.

When *this* summer ended, she was supposed to stay in Toronto, while her mom went home from the cabin alone, back to the comfy cluttered townhouse they'd lived in together for as long as Al could remember.

She flipped pages of the in-flight magazine, through boring ads for jewellery and cars, past articles about places she would never go. She poked and nibbled at a lump of meat buried in gluey sauce. Twice she squeezed past the woman beside her to visit the washroom. She bugged the flight attendant for more pretzels. Using the back of the barf-bag for note-paper and a pencil from her knapsack, she scribbled, *Dear Sam, This sucks.* What else was there to say?

She crumpled her message, shoved it behind the boring magazine, and heaved a disgruntled sigh.

"You seem a little restless," the woman beside her said. "Would you like to try one of these magazines?"

Toronto Life. Vogue. "No, thanks," Al said, but she got the message.

She pulled her sketchbook and pencil crayons from her knapsack. In blue, green, and yellow, she started to plan a design of triangles and circles she could do in paints later. If her dad didn't have a fit about messing up his kitchen.

"Good sense of colour you've got," the woman said.

"My mom's an artist."

"I'd say she's not the only one in the family."

Overlapping blue and yellow gave Al a different shade of green than the green pencil alone. Would that make too many colours in the design? Or should she bring in a complementary orange and really open it up?

The tinny voice on the loudspeaker announced, "We are beginning our descent into Pearson International Airport. Would all passengers please ensure baggage is stowed, seat-belts are fastened, and chair-backs returned to the upright position."

Al bundled her things into her knapsack and pressed her nose to the window. Grey ribbons of concrete threaded through blocks and blocks of red houses and white apartments. Turquoise pools lay scattered among them. And all over, so much green. She always forgot how many trees there were in Toronto.

The CN Tower. The first time she rode up with her dad, he'd been more scared of the height than she was. Beside the Tower, the spaceship-like Skydome, where Joe Carter signed her cast the summer she broke her arm rollerblading.

The buildings and cars loomed bigger and bigger. You could even see traffic lights changing from red to green. When the plane seemed about to land on the highway, Al sat back in her seat.

two

How's my old girl?" Al's dad met her at the bottom of the escalator in his usual holiday jeans and gave her his usual two-armed, lift-her-off-her-feet hug.

"Fine."

"Good flight?"

"Yup."

"Boy, we've sure been waiting a long time for *this* summer, eh?" Other passengers flowed past them. "Alison, I'm so glad you're here."

"Me too." Al smiled. Her dad hugged her again. "Shouldn't we go get my luggage?"

The usual crush of traffic crept along the highway at the top of the city. Summer construction crews were sweating in the dusty sun. In Alberta, at this very moment, Sam and Mandy and Laura would be splashing down the huge new waterslide at the park. Her mom would be at the townhouse, probably trying to find some kitchen utensil she'd forgotten she took to the studio, or repotting some rangy plant.

Her dad steered up the off-ramp. "Shall we make a stop for ice cream?" he asked.

Al smiled. "We always do."

Inside the cool shop, they faced the rows of tubs, moving forward slowly in the line. Pistachio. Raspberry Ripple. Cherry Cheesecake Jubilee. "They've got a great new flavour," her dad said, "full of chocolate, mint, and peanut butter chips. Want to try it?"

"Think I'll stick with my usual, thanks."

Her dad hesitated. "Good idea." Was he feeling as anxious about all this as she was? He turned to the teenager behind the counter. "Two Pralines and Cream, doubles, on sugar cones, please."

By the time they finished their ice cream, they were winding through tree-lined streets, away from traffic lights and stores. Her dad aimed the zapper at the garage door and drove inside. Al's stomach flopped like it had on take-off.

"Why don't you go drop your stuff in the usual place?" her dad said. There was an edge of excitement in his voice.

In the doorway of the den, Al froze. The couch she usually slept on was gone. So were her dad's desk and computer, his heavy bookshelves and fat books. Gone were his leather armchair and the dark plaid wallpaper on the end wall.

In place of all his things was a pine bed, high up like the top of a bunkbed, with a matching desk underneath. There was a dresser and a full-length mirror.

"Remember admiring this furniture up at IKEA last summer?"

"Daddy, I need to use the washroom."

Al splashed cold water on her face. She gulped for air, cupping her hands under the tap. The room. It looked like — she splashed her face again. Like he thought she was going to live here. Forever. Al buried her face in a thick towel.

It was her own fault, if that's what he thought. All those years pretending she wanted to be with him longer, more often. To *live* with him even. She flung the towel against the wall, not caring where it landed.

She'd have to tell him the truth, soon, before he got too set on this idea. She forced herself to breathe deeply, and wet her face once more. She'd tell him soon.

Al hung the towel where it belonged, and went back to the newly decorated room. "So, where's all your stuff?"

"I got someone to build me an office in the basement. I wanted you to have a real room now. Do you like it?"

"It's great, Daddy, I love it." She wrapped her arms around his waist. "Really. It's great."

three

That night, Al climbed up the ladder. Such a stupid way to get into bed. She lay staring at the ceiling.

Was it an hour earlier at home, or an hour later? Or was there a two-hour difference? Earlier. So it wasn't too late to call her mom. Except she'd only just got here. She couldn't call already. Besides, she could hear her dad still tidying up downstairs. Tomorrow would be soon enough to face that look in his eyes again. *Is everything okay?*

Minutes clicked by on the digital clock down on the desk. She kept leaning over the side of the bed to see it. 10:56. 11:34. 12:08. Al crept back down the ladder and sat at the desk. She hadn't unpacked yet, but her dad had put paper and pens and stuff in the top drawer.

July 30

Dear Mom,

How are you? How is Rumplestiltskin? Does she miss me? Daddy's new cat is very unfriendly. I tried to give him a bit of chicken off my plate today but he just walked away, all snobby and superior. Daddy says he probably didn't like the mayonnaise, but I think he's just a horrid cat. His name is Flash, but really he's a big fat lump.

I miss Rumplestiltskin and I miss you.

Love, Allie

She stuck a stamp on the envelope. They were in the desk

drawer, too. Her dad must have thought a lot about things she'd need, or would like to have. There was also a book. *Yours Till Niagara Falls* by Lillian Morrison. It was full of neat ways to end off letters to friends. Nice of him to think of it, but . . .

Al climbed up to bed and slept.

When she woke, the sun was coming in the wrong side of her room. And she was as close to the ceiling as the floor. She remembered where she was. It was too early for traffic noise. Only the starlings in the maple outside her window seemed to be awake. Al crept down the ladder.

July 31

Dear Sam,

I got here yesterday. It feels like longer.

Please promise you'll stay my best friend even if I'm not with you, okay?

Your friend till the kitchen sinks, Al

This was awful. Not being able to just run around the corner to Sam's, or go into the other room to tell her mom an idea for a painting.

She rummaged in the pocket of her denim jacket for the tattered paper she knew was there. She climbed again into her tall bed, unfolded the page she had read a thousand times already, hoping each time that some loophole might have appeared. She flattened it on her pillow.

The mother shall have sole custody of the child, Alison Marie Gaitskill, subject to reasonable access thereto by the father, until such time said child becomes 12 years of age; when, for a period of one year commencing during the summer break subsequent to her birthday, the father shall have sole custody, subject to reasonable

access thereto by the mother. Immediately
following said year, the child shall of
her own accord determine her place of
residence.

For a period of one year. Shall of her own accord determine.

Al clenched the paper in her fist, rammed it under her
pillow, buried her face there, and finally, bawled.

august

four

The truth. What *was* the truth?

Daddy, I love you. I love spending two weeks with you in the summer. I miss you when I'm at home and wish I could see you more often. That was the truth. The truth she had already told him, different times, lots of ways.

Daddy, I love Mommy, even if you don't. I miss her when I'm here. I don't need to live with you for a year to know I want to keep living with her, even though we sometimes argue. That was the truth, too. The truth that would break his heart.

They leaned on the wooden rail of the ferry slicing its way across the harbour. The city shrank behind them. Al's dad, camera slung over his shoulder, rested his foot on their picnic hamper. He was pretty good-looking for someone over thirty. Al liked how the blond hair on his arms curled against his tan, the goofy hat he wore to keep his high forehead from burning. And he had one crooked tooth that showed when he smiled, like her own crooked tooth. But it looked better on him. She tried to imagine her mom falling for him, as she must have years ago, but it was too weird.

The benches on the upper deck were filled with kids, and every one was holding a teddy bear. Except the littlest one whose teddy was a rabbit. "Is there a Teddy Bears' Picnic today?" Al asked him.

The boy buried his face in his dad's thigh. "There is," his dad said, "but he's a little worried that rabbits might not be allowed."

"Maybe you should have brought your teddy," Al's dad teased.

She smiled. They'd gone to a Teddy Bears' Picnic at the Island once. She still had the picture taken five years ago of her and Skiff in their wagon at the end of a hot, weary day. She hadn't brought Skiff to her dad's in ages. She might have this time, if she intended to stay. She would have brought her Alannis tapes, too, and the Kurt Browning poster from her bedroom wall.

Sailboats glided in front of the ferry and behind as it chugged across the harbour. There was enough wind to blow away the summer smudge that usually hung brown over the city. Today you could see clear past the top of the CN Tower. Rippled reflections of blue sky and office highrises shone off mirrored buildings. "Can we see where you work from here?"

"See that — "

H-O-N-K! The horn announced their arrival at the dock. Seagulls squawked out of the way. The boat shuddered to a stop and people started to pile off. In front of them a girl complained to her mother, "But last night you said we'd be back in time for Jenn's party." Al wondered what her mom did last night.

"Paddle boats today or bikes?" her dad asked.

"I don't care. You decide."

"Whatever makes you happy."

To go home like usual at the end of August. That's what would make me happy. "Paddle boats," she said.

Maybe today she could tell him. After a couple of hours, when he was more relaxed. *Daddy, you know what?* she would say. *I don't really need a whole year to decide. I want to go home now.*

"One paddle boat for two hours," her dad told the young woman at the rental counter. He pulled a twenty dollar bill from the wad in his wallet to leave as a deposit.

Al's mom never had money like that, not even at the beginning of the month. Sometimes she even had to put groceries back when she got to the checkout, because she'd run a little short. No wonder she complained all the time that he never sent enough.

They pedalled lazily through the lagoons and under bridges teeming with people. Ducks played hide-and-seek between the branches of trees that dipped to the water's edge. On the shore were kids playing Teddy Bear games. Around a quiet corner a couple lay in the grass feeding each other pieces of mango.

"I like it here, Dad."

"We can come over in the off-season this year. It's nice without the summer tourists."

"I've been thinking . . . " She watched her sandals pushing the boat pedals, up down, left right, up down.

Her dad reached over and squeezed her hand. "There's lots we can think about doing this year. Isn't it great not to feel pressured by our usual time limit?"

"Yeah. But — "

"We should go pick out paint for your room sometime before school starts. I would have had it done before you came, but I didn't want to decide on a colour without you."

Al nodded. "Thanks."

"Sorry, honey, you were going to say something."

"I forget now."

They paddled back to the rental place and wandered along the shore facing the city till they found an empty picnic table. Al set out everything in its "traditional" order: apples, cake, carrot sticks, sandwiches. She invented the "Backwards Picnic" when she was little, after once talking her dad into letting her start with dessert.

After lunch they strolled across the island to the beach, weaving their way among cyclists and rollerbladers and other walkers. Barefoot in the grass, they threw a frisbee back and forth. In the shade of a maple, they spread a blanket. Al pulled a book from her bag that her mom had tucked in at the airport, a collection of short stories. "Isn't it cool how the cover's split in blue and black and then the face is also split in blue and white?"

"If you like that sort of thing. I like a face to look like a face."

"Well, it's a mask, right? I like it." She scanned the titles on the contents page. "Want me to read to you, Dad?"

She lay on her stomach and read aloud. He stared into the leafy canopy above them, listening. "It's amazing," she said when she finished the story, "how writers can make pictures with words that you can see almost as clearly as painted ones." She tickled a piece of grass across her dad's stomach where his shirt gaped.

"Here," he said, "let me read one now." He sat up, cross-legged, flipped through the pages, and started to read: "You know that your problems are all of your own making?"

Yeah right. But soon she was caught up in the problems of a girl in a future society where water was rationed and you had to have a permit to have a baby, only this girl didn't and some official told her the best thing for her to do was apply for euthanasia.

When they strolled back to the ferry dock, the low sun reflected off city windows and seemed to set the buildings on fire. The boat chugged across the water. A flock of tired bodies flowed down the ramp and through the gates of the terminal. Heat still rippled off the pavement.

"Spare change?" A stubbly-bearded man with one arm held out a dirty baseball cap. Al tucked herself into her dad's side.

In the car, she leaned her head back against the leather seat. If only it could be summer holidays forever. Then she'd never have to tell him all she really wanted to do was go home.

five

There was a letter on the mat inside the door. Al took it to her room and tore it open.

August 16

Dear Al,

How are you? I miss you already. We went to the water park on the weekend. It wasn't the same without you.

My mom says any judge who thinks it's fair to force a kid to decide which parent to live with should be locked up. Besides, who'd want to live in some smelly big city full of pollution and drug addicts anyway? Especially with a dumb dad who had to do some stupid custody fight.

You better be home in time for us to start Coulee Junior High together, like you said.

Your best friend, (don't worry), Sam

Al shoved the letter in the bottom drawer of her desk.

Later, when her dad was outside watering the grass, Al went to his basement office and shut the door. She punched in her phone number.

"Hi. Mom?"

"Sweetie, how are you?"

"Okay."

"What have you been up to? Are you having a nice time?"

"I wasn't sure if you'd be home today or at Aunt Karen's cabin."

"I'll go tomorrow. I decided I might as well get my studio set up for my fall classes first. It won't be as nice up there without you though."

"Yeah."

"I ran into Sam at the mall this afternoon. She says to say hi."

"What was she doing? Was she with anybody?"

"She and some other girls were picking up school supplies. School starts back earlier here than in Ontario. So you'll have an extra few days of holidays. What do you think you'll do?"

"Mm, Daddy's probably going to drag me to some computer show or something."

"Ah, sweetie, can't you just tell him you're not interested?"

"Yeah, but he'll probably make me go anyway. Mom, I think I just heard him come in from the garden, so I better go, 'kay?"

"I love you, Allie."

"Me too, Mom. Bye."

Al went to the kitchen and poured herself a glass of milk. In the living room, her dad was watching the news. Even though he was relaxed, his shirt was tucked in, the crease in his shorts sharp.

"Did that guy just say something about bag ladies?" She sat down to watch, too.

"Mmhm." The ice cubes clinked in his glass.

"Is that like the Lunch Bags at Casey who supervised at lunchtime? What would they ever do to get on the news? Steal some kid's sandwich?"

He smiled. "They're trying to pass a new bylaw to keep beggars from harrassing people on the street. They sometimes refer to the women as bag ladies."

"I thought beggars were just men."

"No, there are women, too. Awful, really."

"I don't get why they call them bag ladies."

The little thinking-V in his forehead deepened. He sipped his drink and pursed his lips as if he didn't like the taste. "They drag filthy bags around with them everywhere they go, full of everything they own supposedly."

"Uck."

"I try not to think about it. You should, too. Say, would you still like to go to that Computer Show tomorrow?"

"Yeah. For sure."

"And maybe we can pick up that paint for your room, too."

september

six

Masses of kids Al didn't know and didn't want to know streamed through the halls. She kept her eye on the back of a red shirt she was sure belonged to someone in her class and followed it into a room. She stopped. None of the faces looked at all familiar. Besides, her timetable said Art was next and this was clearly the Science room. She fought her way against the flow and back into the hall where only a few stragglers wandered to classes.

Al pulled her timetable from her binder. Art. Room 214. Hadn't she been in Room 214 before? She looked at the door she'd just come out of — Room 114. Hunched around her books, she scuttled like a frightened prairie dog to the stairs. The second floor hall was empty.

The teacher had already started. "Art is life and life is art." Al stopped in the doorway. Thirty pairs of eyes bored into her. Ms. Pickles — her home room teacher — turned and focused huge round glasses on the latecomer. Orange hair bobbed at the top of her tall skinny body. "As you can see I start my classes on time. Please arrange to get here more quickly next time."

"Sorry, I got lost. Sort of."

"Come in. There's a seat down the middle of this row." Al slunk down the aisle through a buzz of voices, her face burning. If she'd got here in time, she could have picked the back corner like she had in other classes. Ms. Pickles droned on about self-expression and knowing yourself.

On the back of a notebook Al sketched a quick caricature. It looked like a pipe cleaner fuzzed out at the top. When someone came by to hand out drawing paper, she tucked the cartoon inside her desk.

"Let's see?" the girl said.

Al shook her head. "It was nothing."

"No, it was cool."

Al shrugged.

"Now," the pipe cleaner chirped, "I'm going to put on some music. I want you to just listen. Just listen, until I tell you to start drawing. The subject will be yourself. While the music plays, I would like you to create a self-portrait."

Why did they always have to do that? Why couldn't they just let music be music and art be art? Why did they have to go trying to mix them together like that? And could there be a more boring subject to draw than yourself?

The violins jangled her at first, till strains of flute joined in. Then piano chords pittered down and after a soft slow moment, the frantic pace of the whole orchestra filled up everything. In bold confident strokes the oil pastels moved across Al's blank sheet. She was vaguely aware in some corner of her brain of changing colours, tipping the oily sticks on edge, of grinding them down to flat nubs, but mostly she was lost. When the music stopped she rubbed sweat from her forehead with her wrist.

She glanced quickly around, almost surprised to find herself in school. Her fingers were smeared with colours she had no memory of choosing. Had the music been playing for two minutes or twenty? Had she been doing something dumb, like humming along?

Everyone else was looking at their papers. Good.

The drawing on her own desk was nuts. Her long straight hair and bangs were there, but she must have grabbed a purple pastel by mistake. In the middle of the page was a tiny little blue and white collar like the one on her navy sweatshirt, but what was this mess of flamboyant splotches?

She'd never owned anything like it, and wouldn't want to. And what was with these sleeves? Bold stripes seemed to yank her arms straight out from this wild outfit and off the sides of the paper. Such garbage.

"Some fascinating technical challenges met here," Ms. Pickles said from behind her.

"Not on purpose," Al mumbled.

"And such a unique perspective. Why do you suppose you see yourself like that?"

"I don't. This is just stupid."

"I see someone torn about a difficult situation. Very expressive."

A boy in the next row said, "I'm torn all the time. Like, should I go see *Terminator 3* this weekend or *Naked Gun 4*? Should I ask Beth to go with me? Or maybe the New-girl?" He changed his tone to make New-girl sound like something real hot. Everyone laughed. The bell went to end class.

"Alison, would you stay behind for a moment, please?"

Lockers banged in the halls. Kids shouted. "I apologize," Ms. Pickles said, "for drawing attention to you as I did. I should have realized it would not be welcome." Al shrugged. "But you are a talented artist." She held out a brochure. "You might find this interesting. I'd like you to take it home to your parents. Or, rather . . . it's your father you're living with, isn't it?"

"Thanks," Al mumbled. She shoved the brochure inside a notebook and rushed off. She was not about to be last into class again.

seven

A l clung to the sides of her tray. There was nowhere
to sit. The rows of cafeteria tables were filled with
noisy pairs and groups of three or four chatting and laughing, ripping open lunch bags, clattering down trays.

It was stupid to have started school here, planning, after
a week or two, to use some rotten teacher as an excuse to
go back to Alberta. *I just can't learn Math from this guy, Daddy.
Staying here could jeopardize my entire future.* Trouble was her
dad was too smart to fall for a line like that and she was
too chicken to say outright what she wanted.

"Hey, New-girl, wanna sit with us?" The boy from Art
class. Beside him his friend grinned. "Really," he said,
"don't mind him."

Near the back of the cafeteria, at the end of a table, was
an empty seat. Al made a bee-line for it. She chewed her
sandwich slowly. It was hard to feel invisible sitting alone.
She fished the Art teacher's brochure out of her notebook.
It gave her something to look at besides the food fight
happening at the other end of the table.

On the cover was an impressionistic picture of the Art
Gallery of Ontario. She'd been there once. They had tons
of neat art there — Henry Moore sculptures, Group of
Seven paintings. Her dad found it boring, but she loved
the red room with paintings crammed in almost floor to
ceiling. She never knew the Gallery held classes though.
That's what the inside of the brochure was about. Art classes

for adults in the evenings, for kids on Saturdays or after school.

Al read student comments and compared samples of their work to what she knew she could do. She longed to say to someone who would understand, imagine painting and sculpting and drawing right there under the same roof as all that famous art. But none of the animals at this school would know a paintbrush from a fig newton.

She wouldn't be taking the classes anyway. They'd cost a fortune and her dad would never see the point. Besides, with any luck she wouldn't be around long enough to bother starting.

After school, Al hugged her homework to her chest as she ambled along the residential street. Most of the kids had already disappeared in chummy groups. Up ahead a girl in her class was walking by herself. Dark curls bounced on her shoulders and a long print skirt flicked at her knees. Weird. She turned along a crescent leaving Al alone, except for a mom with a stroller racing in the opposite direction, her eye fixed on some far-off place.

The houses Al passed were old and close together. There was no one around any of them. Not like at home where there'd be neighbours gardening and kids playing hop-scotch or hide-and-seek. Squirrels argued and chased up and down trees that made the street feel dark, especially on a dull day. Why would anyone want to live here?

Al stuck her new key in the lock of the heavy wooden front door. It was the first time coming in without her dad being there. The only mail on the mat was some bills. Nothing from home. Flash tiptoed round the corner from the kitchen, flicked his tail, and strutted back out of the room.

"Same to you." She plunked the mail on the coffee table, bare except for the TV remote, and an African violet absolutely in the middle. She flicked a leaf that should have been fuzzy. Fake. At home any table would be crowded with magazines, sketches, dishes of munchies, sprawling living plants. The whole house was like that — crammed with bargain furniture her mom couldn't resist refinishing, half-finished collages and found-object sculptures. This almost-bare house, especially with no one in it but her, was almost creepy.

Tick, tick, tick. The chrome clock on the wall unit.

If she had any guts, she'd be over at Sam's or Mandy's now, making brownies, or else out riding in the coulees. Or maybe she'd be at the pottery studio, if there was a free spot in any of her mom's classes, and there usually was. She could see her mom bent over the wheel, a wisp of dark hair falling across her face as her hands guided the wet clay beneath her fingers. She could feel it running smooth against her own palms, smell the earthy room where she'd spent hours chatting quietly with her mom and her students, later picking clay out from under their fingernails.

Where were the things she'd made and given her dad for Christmas over the years — the little dishes and pottery creatures? There were a few ornaments in the wall unit, mostly expensive pieces of glass. She stood on tiptoe. At the back of a shelf she found the lumpy little clay cat with wire whiskers she'd made when she was in Grade Four. She took it to her room where it would be appreciated.

Back downstairs she clicked on the TV and opened her Math book. The AGO brochure fell out. She studied it again. When she went to the kitchen for a glass of milk, she left it on the counter. She grabbed a handful of cookies from the cupboard.

Time passed quickly as some soap opera babe broke it to her guy that they had to stop seeing each other. She'd discovered they were brother and sister, and besides, she had decided she really loved this hunk who only had six months to live, and before he died she had to get him off his murder charge.

"Did you bring this home, Alison?" her dad called from

the kitchen. She'd hardly noticed him come in.

"What?" She clicked off the TV. "Oh, that. Yeah. My Art teacher thought I might be interested."

"And?" He brushed cookie crumbs off the counter and into the sink.

"I don't really think — "

"You must miss going to your mom's studio, don't you?" He loosened his tie and undid his top button.

"Well, yeah."

"Seems these classes might be just the ticket for someone as keen on Art as you are."

"Um, well . . . yeah."

"Which day do you think?" He skimmed the schedule.

"You don't mean I can go, do you?"

"Why not?"

Because I want to go home as soon as you can get me a flight and the classes don't start till the beginning of October? But he looked so happy to be offering her this chance. And it was the chance of a lifetime. Again she pictured herself in a spattered smock holding her paint brush to an easel, the great masters hanging all around her.

"You name the day, we'll get you registered tomorrow."

"Tuesday?"

"Sounds good."

"What time will you pick me up at school? I'll have to be at the Art Gallery at four thirty."

Al's dad stared at her. He didn't speak. Had he changed his mind? Or had she sprouted a humungous zit in the middle of her forehead?

"Alison," he said, "I work until 5:30. I can't just drop everything to get you to a class." He stuck a bowl of ratatouille in the microwave, like it was no big deal he'd as good as dumped it on her mental watercolour of herself.

Al headed for her room. She knew it wouldn't work. She'd known it all along. And who cared anyway?

"You can always take the subway down, you know," her

dad called.

"By myself?"

"Lots of kids younger than you take the transit every day. It's not difficult."

Al slipped back into the kitchen, her head filled with images of pick-pockets and gangs and getting pushed onto the tracks and taking the wrong train and ending up way out in Scarborough.

"If you want to take this class, it's the only way." He handed Al a head of lettuce.

She looked at it. "Oh! You want me to do salad?"

To learn to paint where Picasso and Michaelangelo hung, would it be worth the risk of being mugged?

"I wouldn't expect you to do it, Alison, if I didn't think you could handle it."

Al ripped up the lettuce. Nothing more was said till they sat down to eat.

"So, tell me about your teachers." Her dad stabbed an artichoke heart. "Do you have any homework?"

Al pushed chunks of tomato to the side of her plate. "I have to pick a book to read for a novel study."

"What kind of computers do you have at school?"

"I don't know."

"I hope they're good enough for you to learn something useful. They're the way of the future. And you know what they say."

"Yeah, I know. The future is now."

"Tell you what, kiddo." He ground extra pepper across his salad. "How about on Saturday we go to the library and get you a book for that novel study. Then we'll go downtown. I've got work to do and it'll give you a chance to get to know your subway route."

eight

Dear SAM,

I am writing this letter on one of the computers at my dad's work. As you can see, I am still "HERE".

Isn't it cool all the different FONTS **there are to pick from.** *Computers can do so many things!*

Like, for 2 hours I've been playing with a program Metroplan uses for something to do with city block layouts or something. The graphics are great. I've heard of doing math and writing at the computer, but a person could actually be a computer artist. If my dad will give me a big envelope, I'll send you a printout of the designs I've made.

How are things at Coulee? My new school (for now) is weird. You can only go to the library when your timetable says, and most teachers make us sit in rows. My teacher's name is — get this — Ms. D. Pickles. She says the D stands for Doris. I don't think anyone believes her.

One good thing. My dad signed me up for a class at the *Art Gallery of Ontario.* (Don't worry. They only run for 10 weeks.) To get there I have to take the subway downtown by myself. If you don't hear from me in a while, I'm probably

LOST UNDER TORONTO!

Your friend till the pencil case gets solved, Al

october

nine

Butterflies had a field day in Al's stomach all through her Tuesday afternoon classes. For the fiftieth time that day she reached into her pocket. Yes, her subway ticket was there. The bell rang and she headed for the door. She hurried past two- and three-storey brick houses, the apartment building on the corner, and over to Yonge Street where shoppers bustled and traffic crawled. Usually she liked to check out window displays in the stores, but today she aimed straight for the red and white sign at the entrance to the subway.

An unshaven man in rumpled clothing sat at the top of the stairs with his hand out. Al veered to the opposite side.

Once underground, she concentrated on the signs. South. She had to go south. She found the right platform and stood back from the edge to wait for the train. Other passengers clutched their briefcases and expensive-store bags. On a sign hanging over the platform little red lights flashed off and on to create moving messages. RIDE THE ROCKET — TTC — THE BETTER WAY . . . PROBLEMS? NO ONE TALK TO? CALL THE KIDS HELP PHONE 1-800-868-6868.

Al turned her back against a gust of smelly fumes as the train rattled into the station. Quickly she checked again that she was on the southbound platform, and stumbled with the crowd through the nearest door. The whistle blew. She grabbed a seat.

A few stops later, the platform was crowded with passengers.

Many on the train stood to leave. Was this her stop? She twisted in her seat to read the station name on the yellow tiled wall behind her. Bloor. She studied the map above the door. Of course. This was where the two lines crossed. She could go three more stops and get off at Dundas, or stay on and loop around past Union Station and get off at St. Patrick. It was also on Dundas Street but closer to the Art Gallery.

She decided on the route that would keep her on the subway longer. It was interesting to watch the people, hard not to stare at some of them. Like the black woman across the aisle with her hair done in hundreds of tiny braids. Al sometimes wore hers in one heavy braid down the back. But these must have taken hours, and how would she ever get them out? And there was the mother not much older than she was, too, slapping her little boy every time he stood up to look out the window. And the guy with tattoos on every inch of both arms and crawling out the neck of his pink satin shirt.

Al fingered the pencil in her pocket. Her knuckles rubbed against the coil back of her mini-sketchbook. But in such close quarters, she didn't dare take them out.

A few more times, the train stopped. At every station people herded through the doors, out and in. Each time she craned her neck to see the name on the wall and checked the map above the door. The train rocked through the dark tunnel. The next stop was St. Patrick.

Al jostled her way between passengers and squeezed out the door. She followed the crush upstairs to the street, then stopped. Which way? Which of these incredibly wide streets was Dundas? "C'mon kid, move it." She felt herself nudged to the curb.

"Find the Legislature," her dad said, "to get your bearings. It's a big building, kind of pink, that looks plonked down in the middle of the road, and that's north. Or find the statue that looks like Gumby in the middle of University.

That's on the south side of Dundas. Once you know north or south, it's easy to figure out west, the way you want to go. And if you get mixed up," he said, "you can always ask someone."

Right.

The big government building at the end of six lanes of traffic. And Gumby.

Skirting another panhandler in a doorway, Al hurried along the sidewalk. Kids were polishing the huge sculpture on the corner with their coat sleeves. When she saw it, she knew she was there. She'd made it.

The classes were in the basement. Smells of paint and charcoal dust filled the room where she and nine other kids pulled on old shirts. Right away the teacher invited them to choose from the overflowing shelves anything they'd like to use for their first project. Dried flowers, old shoes, plaster casts, bottles, costumes, watering cans, bricks, styrofoam blocks and balls, feather boas — all kinds of wonderful shapes and textures spilled into the room.

"Can we pick more than one thing?" asked one of a pair of twins.

"Up to you," the teacher said. "I'm giving no direction at all on this one. I want to see where your strengths and weaknesses are before we get down to serious play. Choice of media and size of paper is also up to you."

Too many decisions. But something about the old-fashioned toaster, all chrome and bulgy, appealed to her. And the bottle brush and feather duster. She stood them up where bread was supposed to go, and settled on black and white conté to capture it all. It was nonsense, but something about this teacher's style — his mismatched socks? the spoon tucked behind his ear? — told her nonsense would probably be okay.

They worked for half an hour, then went upstairs to the Gallery itself. The teacher stopped them in front of different paintings. "Where does your eye go first in this one?"

he asked. "And how does the artist draw your eye to that aspect of the composition?" He invited them to roam and answer those questions about other paintings they especially liked. Al itched to get back downstairs to try out what she was seeing.

Soon they did — chose three objects from the shelf, and sketched out several roughs that would each lead the eye differently.

"That's all we have time for, folks. Next week, you can work up the sketch you decide is most pleasing."

"Sir, can I ask why you've got a spoon behind your ear?"

"Ah!" He reached into the pouch of his sweatshirt, like a magician pulled out a little tub of yogurt, and flourished the spoon. "Snacktime, of course."

Al stored her black and white conté toaster, flew down the steps, and back along Dundas to the subway. She couldn't wait to write Sam and tell her all about it, couldn't wait till next week's class.

ten

"Hi, Sweetie, how are you doing?"

"Mom! Okay, I guess."

"I called earlier but you weren't home yet."

"I had to go somewhere."

"To a friend's? Are you making friends now?"

"No. Daddy signed me up for something downtown."

"Downtown!"

"Yeah, I get the subway after school. I thought I'd be too scared, but — "

"Well, of course. You shouldn't be by yourself in the subway. Can't you take a cab? Your father can certainly afford to send you safely. If you really must go downtown."

Actually, Mom, I love taking the subway. It makes me feel like someone new, someone in charge and competent. "I'll ask him about the cab."

"What is it you have to go all the way downtown for anyway?"

"Just this class."

"What kind of class?"

"Art."

"I see. Well, you should like that quite a lot."

"It's okay. It's not that good, really."

"Hm, too bad. But next year you can get back into your work here at the studio, eh?"

"Yeah. I wish it could be sooner."

"I know. Sweetie, I know."

eleven

Al scuffled along the street through crunching leaves. So many fell in such a short time here. She'd raked up a huge pile last week and already it looked like the job had never been done. She actually didn't mind raking. Every scritchy sweep felt so productive and she liked the mouldy earthy smell. But it made her feel sad, too, for some reason she didn't understand.

At the house across from her dad's, a little boy with his own rake was following his mother around as she tried to clear their front lawn. He dropped his rake, flung himself to the ground, and yelled, "Cover me up." His mom piled leaves on top of him. He jumped out of the pile with a great roar, then lay down again. "Cover me up again." His mom again piled leaves on top of him. "Where did Ryan go?" She called across to Al, "Have you seen Ryan?"

Al played along. "I haven't seen him anywhere," she answered. "Where can he be?"

The pile of leaves erupted in an explosion of little boy blue. Ryan hurled himself into the air laughing.

Al fished in the pocket of her jeans for her key. Now why did a silly thing like that make her homesick? She'd never even raked leaves with her mother. And yet she had to swallow around a lump as she unlocked the door to her father's empty house.

"Meow."

She scooped the handful of mail from the floor, spotting

right away Sam's return address. "I'll feed you later." She nudged Flash outside with her foot, and without even bothering to take off her jacket, tore open the fat envelope.

October 11

Dear Al,

You take the subway downtown by yourself? Way to go! I joined Art Club. Not that you'll think that's such a big deal, now that you're going to the A-G-O — la-de-dah. If you ask me, your dad sent you there because he doesn't want it to look like there's anything your mom would give you that he wouldn't. Jason is in Art Club too. And he's not going with Angela any more.

Things at Coulee aren't that different from Casey. Even Miss Lennon is at Coulee now. She transferred and all the same girls who had her in Grade 5 are in her homeroom. Except you! Rats!! I can't believe you got stuck with a teacher named Dill Pickles.

The Thanksgiving weekend weiner roast was the best one we ever had. 347 weiners got cooked. That's $694 for United Way. After all the little kids and grownups went home, except for chaperones, I stayed for the dance. It was mostly Grade 8s and 9s but Sunita, Laura, and Mandy stayed too.

Remember the quiet blonde guy who won the anti-smoking poster contest last year? He asked me to dance. Twice. I think he would have walked me home, but my mom came to pick me up.

Last week my brother started working at that hamburger place across from the school. I said, "Don't you know how much garbage that place dumps into the world? Don't you know every one of their styrofoam containers will sit in a landfill site for more years than you'll be alive?" But he's such a slug. He just said, "It's not my fault so many people want hamburgers," and

*picked another zit off his ugly face. Brothers! Who needs
them?*

*I guess your dad's making you stay the whole year,
eh? RATS!!*

Your friend, Sam

Al chucked her jacket on a chair, poured herself a glass of
milk, and took Sam's letter to her room. She should have
been at that dance. She kicked aside a mound of dirty
laundry and flicked on the radio.

Such a geek Sam's brother was. But right now having
any kind of brother seemed a pretty nice idea. He'd be
someone to talk to about this time at their dad's, missing
all the good stuff, someone who'd know both their parents
well enough to understand — well, everything. Maybe if
she'd had a brother, her parents wouldn't have fought so
much about who she was going to live with. They could
have just gone "a kid for you, a kid for me" and lived
happily ever after.

Al read Sam's letter again before changing into her
sweats. She dropped her jeans on the cans of paint in the
bottom of the closet, the cornflower-blue paint she and her
dad had bought for her room.

twelve

Al staggered out to the kitchen, Sunday-morning-bleary eyed.

"You're not planning to wear that today, are you?"

She stretched her sweatshirt and looked at it. "What's wrong with it?"

"Aside from the frayed cuffs and the mustard stain," her dad said, "not a thing. And can't you do something with your hair?"

Al gathered her mop and flopped it behind her shoulders. "Why? It's not like we're going anywhere."

"Have you forgotten? Susan and her daughter are coming over."

"Now?"

"After breakfast. Why don't you go change while I make you an omelette?" He swallowed the last of his coffee and got eggs from the fridge. "And Al?" he called to her as she trudged back upstairs. "How about cleaning up some of your mess while you're up there?"

"Maybe I'll just go back to bed."

"What was that?"

"Nothing. Don't put mushrooms in my omelette, 'kay?"

Al poked her fork around her plate. She wasn't used to a big breakfast, or very hungry. And not at all keen on meeting Susan.

"She's just a friend from work," her dad said.

"Fine. Why do I have to meet her then?"

"You don't, but her daughter Natalie's thirteen. You don't seem to do much with people your own age. Are you finding it hard to make friends?"

"No." *I'm not making friends here because what would be the point? Eight months to go and it's back to the prairies for this girl.*

Eight more months. It was a long time, but she was such a chicken, she'd just have to stick it out. Maybe he'd figure she was going back eventually anyway, if she dropped enough hints. Like, if she never felt like painting her bedroom.

"Looks like a perfect day for our bike hike, eh?"

"Hm? Yeah."

In the ravine the sun was shining. Natalie's close-cropped curls almost matched the reds and oranges of the leaves, like flames against the blue sky. She seemed as lukewarm about this outing as Al, which made her a whole lot easier to tolerate than if she'd been happy about it.

Al's dad and Susan pedalled fast and soon left the girls behind. "Do they ever go out, do you think, like on dates?" Al asked.

"That's gross. Our parents? I mean, my mom's got some grey hair. And your dad's not exactly . . . well, no offence, but . . . "

"I know. But some old people go out. I just wondered."

"Well, they don't when I'm around," Natalie said, "but I only live with my mom half the time so I wouldn't know as much as you." They moved over to give a family biking in the other direction room to pass.

"How do you do that — live with each parent half the time?"

Natalie shrugged. "I just do. From Saturday night to Wednesday morning I'm at Mom's then after school Wednesday I go to Dad's and stay till Saturday night."

"Must be nice."

"It helps that they only live four blocks from each other,"

Natalie said. "But you wouldn't believe how often something I need is at the other house, even though they've
tried to set up two complete households. I mean, you're
not going to have two sets of school books, and two sets of
tapes and that, right?"

"Yeah. I didn't know what to do, coming here. Like, I
didn't want to leave stuff in Alberta I might want, but I
didn't want to bring everything either when I'd just have
to take it all back again."

"You mean, you're moving back there?"

"I probably have to stick it out till June, but yeah." Al
flicked a strand of hair out of her face. "You sound surprised."

"Something my mom said, I forget what. But I think she
thinks he thinks you're staying." Natalie laughed. "You
know what I mean."

Up ahead, Al's dad and Susan stopped at a picnic table
by the river. "Please don't tell her what I said, 'kay? My dad
can't know."

Natalie shrugged. "No problem." They coasted toward
Al's dad, crouched beside the table with his camera.

Ten minutes later, he still hadn't put it away. "Dad," Al
objected, "not when I'm eating."

Munching her sandwich, she watched for signs her dad
and Susan might be more than friends. But she didn't catch
any meaningful looks or lingering touches. Too bad in a
way. If the two of them got together, maybe it wouldn't
matter so much when she went back to Alberta.

West was earlier, so Sam was probably just waking up. In
the room where they'd shared so many secrets, including
the medical book that showed stuff they never learned in
Health. Or maybe at somebody else's place. There'd been
a lot of weekend sleepovers happening when she left. A
wave of homesick washed through her with the thought of
Sam, Mandy, Rachel, and probably Sunita or Connie, all
pyjama-cozied into someone's basement.

The camera clicked again. Al sprung from her seat. "I'm going to ride ahead." She took off before anyone had time to object, or try to join her.

thirteen

On Hallowe'en the temperature dipped close to freezing. Al doled out candy and UNICEF money her dad had put in bowls, while he worked in the basement. Probably Aunt Karen would be down from Calgary at her mom's, the two of them dressed as ghosts or witches, scaring all the kids who came to the townhouse door.

Parents huddled on the sidewalk as kids stomped up the stairs to the porch, their costumes almost hidden by warm coats. Most of the kids were little. Hardly any were her age. Not like at home.

Every Hallowe'en since Grade One she and Sam had come up with some kind of twosome act. Once they were the man from Glad and a garbage bag. Another time a pencil and a pink eraser. Another, the tortoise and the hare. Last year, when they went out as Tweedledum and Tweedledee, they had to stop at every other house so Sam could shove Al's tummy-stuffing back into place.

"Hi. I didn't know you lived here." Under white make-up and a sad clown smile was the face of a girl from school. "We could have gone out together."

Al shrugged. "I'm not that big on Hallowe'en myself."

november

fourteen

The wind was raw and damp. Al pulled her collar up around her neck, tucking her chin down inside it. Her mom had said the cold in the east was different from the dry western cold. And was it ever. It seeped right into your bones.

It didn't help that the sun hadn't shone in days.

Al decided to take a short cut through the alley that ran behind some of the shops and restaurants, where she'd be a little more protected from the wind. Yellowed newspapers tumbled past parked cars. Beside one of the many garbage bins stood two small children wearing only light jackets and thin summer pants. They shouldn't be playing back here, Al couldn't help thinking, and didn't their mother care about dressing them properly for the cold?

But they weren't playing and they weren't alone. Reaching into the next bin was a woman, also thinly dressed. Disgust rose in Al's throat. Till the woman, handing the smaller of the children a half-eaten hamburger, raised her eyes, then lowered them quickly when she saw Al watching. The two children began to turn then. Before Al could see their eyes, too, she hurried on as if she had witnessed nothing, had not invaded this family's private indignity.

The look on the woman's face followed her out of the alley to the busy street, and over to the subway. The same man who was at the top of the stairs every Tuesday was there in spite of the cold. Above the old brown blanket wrapped around his shoulders, his cheeks were pink. He caught her eye. Again embarrassment burned through her. There was nothing threatening about this man she was always so nervous of passing. He wanted money, but he wasn't going to rob anyone for it.

Still, most people were ignoring him, so Al did too.

When she got home from her Art class, the smell of beef stew greeted her. Her dad was just stirring in the parsley, listening to the news on the radio.

"The accident that tied up traffic on the Don Valley since early this afternoon has at last been cleared away. One person died in the crash. One was taken to hospital in critical condition."

"Good timing, Alison. Dinner's just about ready. How was your day?"

"Alright." She headed up the stairs.

"Don't go away. I'll be serving this up in about two secs."

Al plunked herself down at the kitchen table.

"Good class?"

"Mhm."

Her dad set down a plate of stew. Steam rose from it and her stomach cried out its hunger. She reached for a slice of bread and dipped it into the hot gravy swimming around the chunks of beef and vegetables. The eyes of the woman in the alley appeared before her.

"You okay?" Her dad sat down with his plate.

Al nodded.

"Eric Nugent," the newscast continued, "aged fifty-four of no fixed address was found dead in the stairwell of a building at Gerrard and Parliament last evening. Authorities say there are now hundreds of homeless people in Toronto, sleeping over subway grates, in stairwells, lobbies, or wherever they can find a bit of warm shelter."

Al pushed her plate away.

"Come on, honey. Not eating won't help anything."

"Maybe later. I'm not that hungry."

"Don't worry too much about this, Alison. A lot of these people want to live that way."

"Not this woman I saw today. She was taking food out of some restaurant's garbage to feed her kids. Daddy, it was awful."

"Where was this?"

"In the alley behind — "

"Haven't I told you not to use those shortcuts?"

Al opened her mouth to speak, but her dad held up his hand to stop her.

" . . . has purchased three more buildings in the downtown core. Plans are moving ahead, company officials say, to tear the old buildings down. Critics of the plan claim this will leave another sixty families without homes. Metroplan's response is 'We will replace these homes with more suitable accommodation.' In sports news tonight . . . "

"Daddy, isn't that your company?"

"It's where I work, yes." He speared another piece of beef and popped it in his mouth.

fifteen

Hey, Alison, want to come for volleyball?"
She glanced up from the sketchbook propped against
her knees. The five other girls in her Outdoor Ed Centre
cabin stood at the door in their sweats. "No, thanks." When
the sound of their voices had drifted away, Al headed
outside by herself.

It was good to be out of the city. She crossed the field to
the woods and found the start of the lake path. Probably
the girls in her class thought she was some snob, never
wanting to do what they suggested. But she couldn't help
it. And besides, she didn't really care what they thought.
Really, she didn't.

The pine needles crunched underfoot. The sky was over-
cast. Did the sun never shine in Ontario? Trees were nice
— trees were great — but some wide open blue sky sure
would lift a person's spirits. Or a letter from Sam maybe.
She hadn't heard from her in weeks.

Maybe Sam was mad because it was November and Al
still hadn't come home. But it was hard to explain stuff to
Sam. Her parents lived together, and she had a brother.
So, how could she understand what it was like — really —
to be an only child of divorced parents? Trying all the time
to keep them both happy?

There wasn't much to see on this path. Just trees and
more trees, with the odd view through them to the flat grey
lake. A beaver had been at work on a couple of poplars,

but the teethmarks stopped part way around the trunks
and there was no sign of the beavers themselves. Soon she
was back at the beginning of the trail, with still another
hour to kill before orienteering. Her five cabin mates,
huddled on the bed under hers, stopped talking when she
walked in. She climbed the ladder past them. As she flopped
onto her mattress one of the girls laughed.

Why couldn't she be in her own room, away from this
snotty bunch? In her own bed above her desk, snuggled
under the quilt crocheted by her mother's mother. Al held
her eyes shut tight till the tears she felt threatening passed.
Then she opened them in surprise. The room she'd been
longing for wasn't one room, but a mix of her room at her
mom's and her room at her dad's. Funny, her dad's place
didn't feel like home when she was there, but where home
was was getting all mixed up in her head. Like nowhere
was really home anymore. Like she didn't really belong
anywhere.

Maybe she should write to Sam. That would make her
feel better.

Dear Sam.

Below her, the girls yacked on about boys and teachers and
makeup.

*Here I am at Claremont Outdoor Education Centre
having the time of my life. Wish you were here.*

Or maybe it wouldn't. Sam wouldn't be missing her like
she was missing Sam. Sam had other friends. She crumpled
her unfinished letter into a ball and pulled her deck of
cards from the pouch beside her pillow. Snap, snap, snap,
she laid out seven cards. Snap, snap, snap, the row on top.
Solitaire. The same stupid game she played in the cafeteria,
and whenever she had nothing she felt like drawing.

From across the field, the bell called everyone to the
central auditorium. Al waited till the others cleared out of

the cabin, then headed over by herself.

When the three days finally ended, a letter was waiting. A letter from her old friend, her best friend! Yeah, how about your only friend.

October 31

Dear Al,

Tonight Mandy and I are dressing up as a dish and a spoon, Connie and Laura will meet up with us dressed as a cow and a moon, and Sunita and Rachel will be the cat and the fiddle. Instead of "trick or treat" we'll shout "hey diddle diddle".

It was brilliant. Sam didn't say who would be the little laughing dog, but it didn't matter. Sam had come up with the best costume ever — without her. But surely somewhere in here Sam would say something about missing her, wishing she was there, that things weren't the same without her.

Guess who's getting married. Miss Lennon! Connie and I are planning a surprise shower for her. We bought this gigantic card already and we're getting everybody to sign it. Miss Lennon getting married! Isn't it romantic? The best part is, we're all invited to her wedding.

It wasn't romantic. It was stupid. They'd probably get divorced in a few years anyway. And have some stupid kid they'd fight over, who'd probably get stuck living some stupid place she didn't want to live.

Flash meowed at the door, whining to be let out. Al opened the door. The cat sniffed the cold air and slunk back into the living room. She would never get married, she had decided ages ago. She would live by herself, just her and her cat. A cat like Rumplestiltskin — an acrobatic comedian who loved her. Flash meowed at the back door. Al went and picked him up.

"You don't like it here either, do you?" She wrapped her

arms around the cat's warm body. Flash jumped away,
scratching Al's hand as he leapt. It was just a small scratch,
but as Al sucked away the blood, tears collected.

I better go get ready. Mandy will be here soon. Mom's
going to order us a pizza before we go out.

Your friend, Sam

Thanks, Sam. I miss you, too. That day in July, with the
wave pool, the Twister game, the ride out to the coulees
with her friends — Sam's mention of pizza brought it all
back. It was another world. Another life. It was her life.
And she had to go back.

sixteen

A l riffled through the drawer of her desk. There must be a loophole, some way to get out of staying the whole time till next summer. Because she had to go home. She had to. Before her old friends forgot about her completely. Why, Sam hadn't even mentioned the possibility of her doing the drawing for Miss Lennon's card, and she'd done all the cards for every special occasion since Grade Three. Happy Birthday. Merry Christmas. Get well soon. Congratulations on your new baby!

Here it was. Al smoothed out the page.

```
The mother shall have sole custody...un-
til...12 years of age, when, for a period
of one year commencing...following said
year...
```

There was no loophole. Any more now than the other hundreds of times she'd read this ragged slip of paper. It was like a prison sentence. For a period of one year. Except even prisoners had some chance of getting out early. Why shouldn't she? What had she done wrong except get born to a couple of people who promised to be together forever, then couldn't even stay together long enough to raise their kid?

Well, if her parents could say *Can't do it*, so could she. When her dad came home from work, she'd tell him. *Daddy, I have to go home. I know the court order says I'm supposed to live with you for a year, but I can't. I don't care if it's breaking the law. I've made up my mind.*

Al dumped her homework on her cluttered desk. She had to write a which-way story, using a which-way book from the library as a model. It was due Friday. She should have at least got it started before the Outdoor Ed trip, but had put it off because she'd read one of those books in Grade Four and hated it. Now she poured herself into the assignment — her last at this dumb school.

She didn't realize her dad had come home till he tapped on the open door of her room. "You're working hard," he said.

Al nodded.

"I was thinking — this weekend might be a good time to get your room done, if you could get some of this mess tidied away by then." He nudged a stray sock in the doorway. "That paint has been in the closet for over a month now."

"I guess I've had a lot of homework, and . . . everything." Al forced herself to look up at her father, to face him squarely with the truth. "Besides I'm . . . I'm just really tired."

That night, after a quiet supper, when her homework was almost done, Al went to the kitchen for a glass of milk.

" — make me wish I'd never tried for custody."

She didn't mean to eavesdrop, but with those few words from the living room, she froze, gripping the handle of the fridge door.

"What chance did I ever have, really? After all these years with her mother, it's a wonder she agreed to come out here at all."

Al wanted to slip back to her room, pretend she had heard nothing of this, but she couldn't.

"She does. I can tell."

All her blood must have rushed to her heart, it was pounding so hard.

"No, Susan, I never had a chance."

It wasn't just the anger in his voice that held her in the kitchen. It was the hurt. There was a long silence on his end of the conversation.

"Of course, it's a hell of a spot to put her in. That's what I hated most about this arrangement right from the beginning." He spoke more quietly now. "I wish I could tell her she doesn't have to be here if she doesn't want to be. But, Susan, I know she doesn't. I saw it in her eyes again today. And . . ."

Another silence. It sounded like it might be on both ends.

" . . . I don't want her to go back."

Al slipped back to her room without her glass of milk. Flash lay in the middle of the floor, a dusty ball of string tangled around his paws. Al could hardly stop her fingers from shaking as she untangled him.

seventeen

SALLY'S ROAD

A Which-Way Story by Alison Marie Gaitskill

Page 1

Once upon a time there was a girl named Sally. She was merrily skipping along the happy road of life when suddenly the road forked. Along one road she could see a dark forest. Along the other she could see a lovely field. [To choose the forest, turn to page 2. To choose the field, turn to page 3.]

Page 2

Sally wandered along the road until she came to the forest. It was dark and creepy and scary. She wondered, Do I have to go into this place? She saw between the trees a friendly creature beckoning her. Come, it said. And she did. The branches of the trees grabbed her and she could hear someone she loved far away crying toxic tears of pain, but she could not escape the cruel branches of the trees. They choked her to death.

Far away her loved one drowned in a poisonous sea.

THE END

Page 3

Sally wandered along the road until she came to the field. It was wide open and fresh. She ran ahead full of joy. But there were brambles growing among the silken grasses. They snagged her feet and tripped her. Lying with her face to the ground she could hear someone she loved far away sobbing spastic tears of pain, but she could not escape the harsh brambles. They grew over her whole body and held her to the ground till she rotted.

Far away her loved one sobbed endlessly tears without end.

THE END

eighteen

Days passed, with more solitaire games in the cafeteria, more visits with Natalie whose easy custody setup made her almost unbearable company, more projects at the Art Gallery to lose herself in, more news on the radio about poor people. The number who had to use food banks every month would fill the Skydome twice. She said nothing to her dad about going home. How could she? It would be bad enough in June when she told him. Telling him now would break his heart. True, her mom wasn't exactly happy about her being here. But it wasn't like she expected Al home before the end of June anyway.

One morning Al woke very early. It was dark, almost the middle of the night. She leaned over the side of her bed to look at the clock: 4:53. She tried to get back to sleep, rearranged herself in the bed, and did relaxed breathing like they learned in gym: 5:16. She counted sheep, and then streetcars: 5:30. It was warm between the covers and the house was cold — the timer on the thermostat hadn't told the furnace to come on yet — but she couldn't lie in bed any longer.

Except for the streetlight shining in the windows, the house was dark as she crept in her housecoat down to the living room. She crumpled newspaper into the fireplace and lay kindling across it. She unlocked the back door and stepped out in her slippers to get a couple of logs from the pile. Clouds of her breath hung in the crisp air. Shivering, she carried the logs inside. It was easier than gathering wood on a desert island, but building her fire to get warm she felt a bit like Robinson Crusoe. She struck the match, its rasp loud in the quiet house. Flame snapped at the paper and soon the wood started to crackle too. Al stared into the heart of the fire, her arms wrapped tight around her knees.

Behind her the floor creaked. She expected her dad to say something about being awake so early, or lighting a fire without an adult there, or some other parent-type comment.

"Nice to wake up to a fire," he said, and sat on the floor beside her. "Where'd you learn to lay a fire like that?"

"Watching Mom at Aunt Karen's cabin, I guess."

"I thought maybe you were a Girl Guide."

"No," Al said. "I hate uniforms."

"You should have seen what I wore when I was a Scout. Silly shorts and cap. And knee socks — you wouldn't believe it was possible to make anything as itchy."

"If you didn't like the uniform," — Al put another log on the fire — "how come you went?"

"I had no brothers or sisters, and didn't make friends easily. But I was never that good at entertaining myself either. I needed the Scouts."

They sat watching the fire for a while. Her dad didn't suggest she join Guides or anything and it was funny how good it felt, cozy and quiet and safe, just thinking, the elbows of their housecoats almost touching.

Slowly the flames dwindled. The furnace clicked on and they decided to put just one more log on the glowing embers. The sky began to lighten. Al's dad sent her upstairs for her shower.

In homeroom that day the class talked about raising money for their Nigerian foster child whose parents couldn't afford food and whose community needed to dig a well. The closest drinkable water was ten minutes away. Al wondered if anyone was raising money for the kids begging in the subway last week, or the ones whose mother's eyes still haunted her.

december

nineteen

Alison," Ms. Pickles said as she handed back the which-way assignments, "some of the choices a which-way reader makes must lead to a happy conclusion of some kind." Her fuzzy pipecleaner head was all quivery. "There must be some that do not, of course, to give the story tension. But if all of the choices lead to disaster, the reader will not want to go on." Pickles straightened her glasses and knit her almost invisible eyebrows. "I'm afraid in your story that none of the alternatives leads to a happy conclusion."

"Well, maybe that's just Life." She hadn't meant to say it so loud. But Pickles went on handing back stories as if her outburst was nothing unusual.

When Al wandered into the cafeteria someone was sitting in her spot near the back. A girl from her class. She found another place to sit where she didn't have to see everyone trading desserts and homework, where she could play solitaire without caring who noticed — or didn't.

Red jack to black queen. Someone sat down beside her. Al didn't turn to see who. When there were no more moves to make, she gathered her cards for another game.

"Do you play Kings in the Corners?" the girl beside her asked. It was Kim, the girl who had sat in her spot.

"No."

"Do you want to see how?" Kim was a loner, the only girl in Grade Seven who wore dresses to school. Not the kind of person Al would ever be friends with back home, but mysterious, set apart from everyone else somehow.

She tapped the worn edges of the deck against her palm, then placed it on the table. Kim laid out the cards in the shape of a cross, and showed how to build up suits in the corners while piling them in reverse order on the cross. She handed Al the remaining cards. "Try it."

Al flipped over a black six, a red three.

"Don't forget to build up the corners. Otherwise you never win."

The bell went for next class. "That's not bad," Al said. She tucked the cards into the pocket of her bag. Kim picked up her books and started to walk away. Her loose paisley-patterned dress in beautiful shades of turquoise and green swung, like all her dresses, just below her knees. She turned. "I'll show you another one tomorrow, 'kay?"

twenty

Envelopes, coloured pencils, and scraps of paper covered Al's desk and littered the floor of the alcove under her bed. She snipped a corner from a large white envelope, opened a book, and slipped the envelope-corner over the corner of a page. Too big. She trimmed the triangle and tried it again.

On a scrap of paper she did a rough sketch of Flash sleeping on her bed. He'd figured out he could get up there last week by jumping first to the windowsill and then up. When she had it the way she liked it, she copied the drawing onto the bookmark she was making for her grampa. She snipped tiny pieces of coloured paper to fit the shapes and glued them on.

She didn't know what to give her mom this year. 4:30, Wednesday, so her mom might be home. Suddenly she had to call, right this minute, even if it wasn't cheap rates yet — as if that would matter on her dad's phone bill anyway.

"Allie, it's prime time. Is everything okay?"

"Yeah, I just had to talk to you."

"You're sure everything's alright."

"I wanted to ask you what you want for Christmas."

"Oh, you know anything at all would be just fine."

"Mommy, can I come home for Christmas?"

Sigh. "You know there's nothing I'd like more than that, don't you?"

"So, can I?"

"Sweetie, I'm sure Grampa Gaitskill booked his flight to Toronto weeks ago."

Al squeezed the phone, as if it might change the answer she was getting.

"I'm sorry, really I am. I should never have agreed to let your father keep you there over Christmas. But he kept harping about all the years he had to come west to see you. Well, you know how he can be."

"Could you come, too?"

"To Toronto, you mean?"

"Yeah."

"To get a ticket now would cost the earth, Allie. And I just don't have it. Oh, sweetie, I'm sorry. You do know how much I miss you, don't you?"

Al swallowed. "It's okay."

"I mailed a parcel yesterday to be sure it would get to you in time. So you watch for it, alright?"

"'Kay."

"But don't open it till Christmas."

"I won't."

"And no peeking?"

"'Kay."

Al opened the bottom drawer of her desk and put her grampa's bookmark inside. From between the desk and the wall she pulled two paintings — an abstract design and a more realistic downtown scene. Maybe she could give one of these to her mom. But which?

She had actually seen the "Two Ladies" separately, waiting on corners for lights to change, but put them side by side in one picture to say something about the city. They were painted in bold acrylics against a background blur of buildings and traffic. One woman wore layers of old sweaters, streaky grey pants that were frayed around the ankles, and a red fedora over stringy brown hair. She pulled behind her a bundle buggy that held a wrinkled half-full green garbage bag. The other one wore high heels, a leather skirt and jacket, and a lacy blouse poofing out the front. Her hairdo was stiff with hairspray, but you could tell it was supposed to look all windblown and carefree. She was sort of staring across the street with her pouty lipstick, like she was trying to pretend the shorter woman wasn't there.

This painting was her best. And her mom would like it. She could give the other one to her dad. It was pretty good, too.

Except it wasn't of anything. She'd just played around with different textures and colours in overlapping geometric shapes. Her dad might not understand "Two Ladies" as well as her mom, but he wouldn't get the abstract at all.

So — realististic ladies for Dad, abstract shapes for Mom. All she had to do was get one of those mailing tubes and send it, soon, so it would get there in time for Christmas.

If only she could squeeze herself into one of those tubes.

Al climbed up the ladder to her bed, heaved Flash over the side, then let herself have a little weep. When she heard her dad get home, she tucked the paintings into the space beside her desk, rinsed her face, and went downstairs.

"Alison, hi. You haven't started dinner yet?"

"Oh, I forgot."

"Just one day a week is all you're responsible for. That's not too much, is it?"

"Sorry, Daddy. I got making Christmas presents and completely forgot about dinner. I'll start it now."

Her dad yanked off his tie. "No, let's just go out."

"I forget to make dinner, so you take me out instead?" Al laughed. "And this is supposed to teach me to be more responsible?"

"You're right. I changed my mind." He wrapped his tie around her waist and through the door-handle of the fridge. "Whose presents were you making, by the way, that you forgot about making dinner?"

"Grampa's. And I decided about yours, too."

"Well, in that case, I changed my mind again." He

handed Al her jacket.

"Are you giving Grampa a stack of books again this year?"

"I expect so. It's a tradition, isn't it?"

Yeah but so is Christmas at his place in Calgary, or at Aunt Karen's with Mom. "Did you know that when I was little I thought Grampa lived in a library, 'cause his house was so full of books?" Al zipped up her coat and followed her dad outside. A few neighbours had their lights up already.

"Alison, I hope you don't mind too much that we're not going there for Christmas this year. I just really wanted to celebrate with you here, in our own home. You'll miss seeing your mom, I know, but it's been a long time . . . "

"That's okay." Al shoved her mittened hands in her pockets. "Really, it's fine."

twenty one

The next day a woman from the radio station came to the school to talk to some of the kids and teachers about their fundraising project.

"We're doing stuff to raise money for our school's foster child."

"From Nigeria."

"Like, we're having a bake sale."

"Want to buy a cupcake?"

"And we're selling some of our old toys and junk at a white elephant sale."

"Want to buy a white elephant?"

"Tell me," the interviewer said, "why are you kids going to all this trouble?"

Gregory, the most hot-air-filled jerk Al had ever laid eyes on, said, "People in Canada are over-privileged. They have a responsibility to help people in underprivileged countries."

Without thinking Al jumped in. "And what about the hungry people in Toronto?"

"People in Canada have a responsibility . . . "

"Have you ever been outside your own neighbourhood, Gregory? Don't you know there are people in Toronto who sleep on the streets and rummage through restaurant garbage for scraps to feed their kids? You think you know everything, but I bet you've never even heard of a food bank, have you?"

Gregory stood with his mouth open, like he was looking

around for someone to protect him from this crazy kid.

"Alison's right," Kim said. The girl from the lunchroom. "Our class should organize a food drive. If you want to be in charge of it, Alison, I'll help you."

Someone else chimed in. "Yeah, charity begins at home, right?"

Gregory licked his lips. "But what about our foster child? We can't turn our backs on the Third World just to feed people in Toronto."

"Who says we have to?" Kim said. "Can't we do both?"

"Thanks, kids. I'll try to get something on the six o'clock news." The reporter snapped shut her case and left as thirty kids argued and made plans and suggestions.

Kim said to Al, "Do you want to talk after school about the food drive?"

What had she got herself into? Working with other people? And this would be a big project, too. "I have to see Mrs. Conlin about Math."

"After that then. Meet me in the cafeteria."

Ms. Pickles interrupted. "We'll have to discuss details of this project later. Some of you have Book Buddies waiting."

Al and five other Grade Sevens meandered down the hall. "Way to put a sock in Gregory," one of the boys said. She smiled.

The door of the Grade One classroom was decorated with a giant Santa. His bag was filled with toys painted by each of the kids. "This one's mine," Al's Book Buddy said.

"What a nice teddy bear," Al said. "I like his red bow." Roberto looked up at her. He had the biggest brownest eyes.

Al took him to his favourite place in the library — the bathtub full of cushions. It was his turn to pick a book this week, and he'd brought one she loved to read aloud.

Roberto slid down the side of the tub and read from the cover. "*The Man Whose Mother Was A Pirate*. By Mar . . . "

"Margaret Mahy. Pictures by . . . " Al pointed to the author's first name then the illustrator's.

"Margaret!"

"That's right. Margaret Chamberlain." She turned to the beginning. "There was once a little man who had never seen the sea, although his mother was an old pirate woman. The two of them lived in a great city far, far from the seashore."

Roberto laughed, pointing out the old pirate woman hanging her striped and polka-dot underwear on the clothesline between tall and dingy buildings. As Al read through the story, he pointed out other details in the pictures. "My mommy has a necklace like that."

"Is your mom a pirate, too?"

"No!"

"Mine is."

"She is not." Roberto raised his dark eyebrows, his eyes opening wide. "Is she?"

Al continued reading. Roberto echoed the pirate woman's words. "Glory! Glory! There's the salt!"

Too soon, they got to the last page. "And if you want any more moral to the story than this," Al finished, "you must go to sea to find it."

Roberto sighed. "Vamos al mar."

"Vamos . . . What's that mean?"

"Go to sea. I'd like to go to sea."

"And be a pirate?"

"Mm . . . The sea captain." Roberto pretended to be rowing his big boat.

Al crawled out of the bathtub. "Can you teach me anything else in Spanish?"

Roberto scratched his chin, then patted *The Man Whose Mother Was A Pirate*. "Una buena historia." He scrambled out of the tub and pulled two more books from the library shelves. "Una buena historia. Una buena historia."

"Yes," Al agreed. "A very good story."

At the door of the Grade One classroom, he said, "Hasta luego, mi amigo."

"Hasta luego, Roberto."

twenty two

December 12

Dear Sam,

Today I was kind of late getting home after school. My dad was already here. All he said was, "I need you to let me know if you're going to be late, okay? You can call me at work." Imagine what my mom would do if I didn't get home till almost six o'clock? On the other hand, she never bugged me about my room like he does all the time.

Tomorrow he's going to take the day off work so we can go downtown to do some Christmas shopping. I told him I already made almost all my presents, but he said it'll be fun to look in the windows anyway, and I can help him pick out a couple of things.

I stuck your present in with this letter. It's like what I made my grampa except for the picture. I hope you like it.

You know what I just thought of? I bet my dad wants to get something nice for that Susan. I forget if I told you about her, but don't worry it's no big deal, I don't think.

I bought my Book Buddy a tiny little book he can stick in his pocket. He's this Grade One cutie I do reading with every week and he's teaching me some Spanish.

They should have Book Buddies at Casey.

We're having a food drive at school. I'm making some posters with this other girl, Kim, and we'll get some other kids to make some announcements. I suggested this guy Gregory because he's got such a big mouth. Dill Pickles says this is a good time for this kind of project because people always feel generous at Christmas.

Feliz Navidad!

Your friend till hot dogs have pups,

Al

P.S. I miss you.

twenty three

The branches of the Christmas tree spread to fill the entire corner of the living room. Underneath it, presents — including a big box from Al's mother — waited to be opened the next day. From the ceiling hung garlands of tinsel and bubble-like balls. A fire blazed in the fireplace.

"This tourtière looks fabulous," Susan said. "Did you help your dad make this, too?"

Al nodded.

Natalie nudged her. "Aren't you wonderful!" Her fiery curls were tugged back in a clip.

"A regular Einstein of Domestic Science. I never cooked a thing till a couple of months ago."

"Come on, folks. Let's eat."

Neighbours and friends from Al's dad's work edged slowly toward the buffet, chatting. The house was full of people, but it had never felt lonelier. And tonight her mom was driving up to Aunt Karen's in Calgary. By herself.

"You better not cry, I'm telling you why," all the grown-ups sang. Ryan chimed in louder than everyone, "San-ta Claus is com-ing to town!"

The flash on her dad's camera went off again. When he wasn't taking her picture, he was winking at her from across the room. Al smiled, hoping he didn't notice she wasn't singing.

The weather said it was snowing in the west. She could see it blowing across the highway, all dizzy-making in the dark. Would there be Northern Lights, too, like last year's that seemed specially put on for Christmas Eve travellers?

There had been no snow in Toronto yet. It was freezing rain on the last day of school when the driver from the food bank and Al's committee struggled across the glazed sidewalk with the twelve full boxes her class had managed to collect.

"Rudolph the red-nosed reindeer, Had a very shiny — "

Ding dong.

"Who could that be?" Al's dad said. "It's a little too early for Santa."

Everyone laughed like it was the funniest thing ever said.

"For you, Alison."

"For me?"

At first all she could see was a cloud of breath and the shape of someone bundled up in winter clothing silhouetted against the streetlight. Then the person turned.

"Kim!" Al stepped out of the noisy house to the quiet of the porch.

"Hi," Kim said. "Merry Christmas." She handed Al a present.

> *To my friend Alison from the West. Welcome to the East.*
>
> *Kim.*

It was so cold out Al's hands were shaking, but she didn't feel cold a bit. "I . . . I didn't get you anything," she said. "I didn't know — "

"That's okay. Open it."

It was a deck of cards with I ♥ TORONTO on the back.

"Now you can play double solitaire," Kim said.

"What's that?"

"It's where you play it with a friend." The first snowflakes of the season drifted down between them. Fat fluffy ones. "You better go in now." Kim started down the steps. "You're shivering."

By the time Kim got to the sidewalk, her feet were leaving prints in the snow. Al called out, "Hey, Kim! My friends back home call me Al."

"Merry Christmas, Al!" Kim called back.

Al rubbed away the goosebumps on her arms. In the house everyone was singing. She slipped the deck of cards into the pocket of her jeans and opened her mouth to join them.

"O-oh ti-dings of co-om-fort and joy, comfort and joy,
O-oh ti-i-dings of co-om-fort and joy!"

twenty four

The neighbourhood lay under a blanket of snow when Al woke the next morning. She could tell by the muffle of everything, even before getting out of bed. Her stocking, hung the night before on her doorknob — her dad had insisted Santa would know to look for it there — was bulging. Suddenly twelve years old didn't feel as old as it had most days lately.

Al looked out at the trees heavy with snow, and the street, with only a few tire tracks breaking up the white. She wondered where the alley kids were right now, and if her guy by the subway was in his usual spot. She scrambled into jeans and sweatshirt and tiptoed down to the kitchen.

"Meow."

"Shh." She placed a saucer of milk on the floor.

Breakfast today would be cranberry-orange muffins she and her dad had made. Twelve was more than the three people in her house would need.

She got freezer bags from the drawer. In one she put two muffins. In another she put three. In case someone woke up and discovered her gone, she left a note:

Running a quick errand. Back soon. XXX

She bundled into her boots and coat and slipped outside. She hurried over to Yonge Street and the back alley where she had seen the mother and two children. A cat wound itself around Al's legs, but there was no one else around.

Of course not. At seven thirty on Christmas morning, what did she expect? But she placed the bag containing three cranberry-orange muffins on the edge of the bin, in case someone came round later. She scurried out to the street and along to the subway station.

And he was there. In the doorway of a store nearby, sleeping between sheets of cardboard. She'd never seen this street so quiet, but her pounding heart made up for the missing traffic and crowds of people as she walked closer, slowly, and crouched down. His eyelids fluttered. *Don't wake up.* She placed the muffins beside him and turned to leave.

"What's this, then?" the man shouted. "Eh? S'posed to be some kind of trick?"

Al turned. He'd shed his cardboard and was holding the bag as if it were something she left after walking her dog, if she had one. "They're muffins," she said, but felt like grabbing them and running home. He wasn't even the tiniest bit grateful.

"Muffins!"

"If you don't want them — "

"Course I do. Unless you put something funny in them."

"Why would I do that?"

He chuckled. He was missing a tooth in the front. "I see there's two here. Want to join me?"

"No. Thanks."

He untwisted the tie at the top of the bag, pulled out a muffin, and raised it the way she'd seen people raise glasses to propose a toast. "Cheers." Could this man have done that once, at somebody's wedding or fancy party, all shaved clean and dressed up in a tie?

He took a bite. "Mmm. Your mom make these?"

Al shook her head. "She lives in Alberta."

"Lived there once myself."

"Me too." She wanted to ask him where in Alberta he'd lived and why he came here, but he might get mad if she got too nosey. Besides, the wish to be back there came over her so suddenly she couldn't trust herself to speak of it again.

"Good muffin. Thanks."

Al brushed her mitt across her cheek. "We have dinner around six," she found herself saying. "Would you like to come? We're along there." She pointed. "Number 148."

"Hmh. Whoever you live with would be real pleased about that." He again wrapped his mouth around the muffin.

"My mom invites people for Christmas all the time if she knows they're going to be alone."

"But she's in Alberta, you said. And what makes you so sure I'm going to be alone?" The man flicked muffin crumbs from his rumpled jacket. "Think fellas like me don't have friends?"

"I didn't mean . . . I better get home."

When she reached the corner, he called, "Merry Christmas, Lovey."

Al opened the door to the smell of coffee. "Well, here she is," her dad said.

"Where have you been so early Christmas morning?" her grampa asked.

"Someone's been into these muffins already." Her dad was setting some on a plate. "Pop, was that you?"

"Don't blame me!"

"I took a few," Al said, "to some people I know."

"That girl who came round last night?" Her dad placed the plate in the microwave.

"Just people. Like, there's this guy over by the subway every day. I think it's where he lives."

"That bum? Begging for money for his next drink is all he's ever up to." The microwave beeped.

"Dad, I don't think that's true. And even if it is, then what's the harm in giving him a muffin? It's just possible he might be hungry."

Al's dad sighed. "You're right. But let's not spoil Christmas over it. These people are not your problem, okay?"

"I guess."

Her dad handed her a cappuccino.

"Is this for me?" she asked.

"Sure, if you'd like it."

"Thanks." She licked the cinnamony froth.

"Just don't go giving it away, now."

"Da-ad."

"Let's take breakfast in the living room so we can get started at that tree, shall we?"

Al curled up in the chair by the window. As usual, her dad poked among the presents, ready to play Santa. She was dying to open the one that arrived parcel post the week before, but tried not to show it.

"This is nice, John," Al's grampa said, "being here in your house for a change on Christmas."

Al opened the first present. Three books about a girl growing up in Toronto during the Depression. "Thanks, Grampa."

"I know you don't consider yourself a Toronto girl, yet, but the woman at the children's bookstore near here recommended them."

"Have you been in every bookstore in Canada?"

"No, but I'm working on it."

"Oh, Alison, this is lovely," he exclaimed later. "Just what I've always wanted."

Al sat back on her heels, lapping up the conversation, the same one that took place every Christmas morning with her dad and grampa. The only trouble was she should be leaving them soon to join her mom at Aunt Karen's. But . . . they'd be thinking of her. And there was always next year.

Al's grampa slipped his new bookmark over a page corner. "Come give me a hug, you talented girl."

Al wrapped her arms around his neck and buried her

nose in the spicy smell of his aftershave. "Thank you for the books." She gave her dad a big hug, too. "I love you, Dad."

"Gee, and you haven't even opened your present from me yet."

"Here, you open yours." She handed him a long striped tube. With a big rip, he tore off the whole wrapping. "You have to slide it out."

"Alison, it's . . . " He looked back and forth between the two women in the painting. "This is marvelous. There's a perfect spot for it downstairs in my den."

"I thought you might want to hang it at work," Al said. "You have such big walls there."

"Oh, I think it deserves a place of honour here at home."

Like the cat I made you in Grade Four? "'Kay."

The box from her mom still sat under the tree, like an elephant someone tells you not to think about. Al squeezed the present from her dad. It was large and lumpy, soft like a bag of laundry. "What is this?"

"Open it and see."

She tore off the paper. It was a patchwork knapsack made from gorgeous pieces of tapestry and quilted denim. "Dad, I love it. It's perfect for my books and lunch. And it's got an outside pocket for my key and subway tickets, too." Al ran her fingers over the smooth stitches embroidered on one of the tapestry patches. "It's perfect, Dad. Where did you get it?"

"Susan dragged me to one of those big craft shows downtown. You know, the ones that travel across the country during November and December?"

"How'd you know I like stuff like this?"

"Just a guess," he said, "but I'd noticed your old bag getting pretty worn-looking."

"It's perfect," Al said again. She hugged him again. "Thanks."

Her grampa pushed the last present, the big box, over

to where she was sitting. "One more here." Flash leaped at a trail of sparkling ribbon.

Al slit the tape on the edges of wrapping, opened the box, and reached into the paper crumpled all around the present. She pulled it out — something cloth, something soft.

It was a knapsack, made from quilted denim and tapestry patches. Identical to the one she'd just opened, except the patches were sewn together in a slightly different pattern.

"One for going to school and one for coming home!" her dad joked. "Ha, ha, ha."

Al laughed along. But she had seen the smile shrink from his face, like the smile on a deflated happy-face balloon.

twenty five

By late afternoon, the smell of the cooking turkey filled the house. Her dad had tidied away all the torn wrappings and her grampa was having a little snooze. Al was helping set the table when there was a rap at the door. "I'll get it." She dropped the serviettes she was folding.

Through the little window in the front door, she saw him. With rough hands, her man from the subway was smoothing the wrinkles in his shabby jacket.

It seemed a good idea this morning, inviting him for dinner — before the fuss over the silly muffins. But now he was actually standing at her house, rumpled and unshaven. Even she found it hard to imagine him at their tidy table with cloth serviettes and matching silver.

Maybe if she didn't answer his knock, the man would just leave.

He raised his hand again. She pulled open the door. But what to say? She had to send him away. And, oh god, there was another one out on the sidewalk.

"Hello, Lovey. Wanted to thank you for your invitation." Al managed to smile weakly, but could not make her mouth form words. "And tell you," the man continued, "we're going to the church, my friend and me, for dinner. He says they do a nice one over there. I wanted to let you know so you wouldn't go setting an extra place."

Al nodded. "That's great."

"So, thanks again for your kindness, but you go ahead

and enjoy dinner with your family, alright?"

She felt her dad's presence behind her as she shut the door.

"I cannot believe what I just heard."

"What? Mom and Aunt Karen always invite people in who'll be alone for Christmas dinner."

"Complete strangers, Alison?"

Al shrugged.

"Bums?"

"Daddy, I made a mistake, okay?" Al's face crumpled. "But don't call him a bum. Please?" She fell against her dad's chest then and cried a flood of tears.

He patted her back like when she was little till the front of his shirt was soaked. "Alison, this isn't all about . . . our unkempt gentleman, is it?"

She shook her head, wiped her face dry on her sleeve. Her dad pulled her to him again. "I'm sorry, honey. Really, I am."

january

twenty six

Al tugged her boot lace so hard it snapped. She yelled, "Dad, have we got any laces?" and stomped through the house to find him.

He looked up from the computer screen in his basement den. "I could pick some up today if you'd like. Or you could."

Al shook the frayed piece of broken lace. "I need one now."

"Well, I don't have one now."

Al heaved an impatient sigh and tromped out of the den. "I'll just wear my shoes then." She was on her way out the door when her dad said, "You could take a lace out of one of my boots."

"Forget it. I don't need boots anyway."

Mounds of dirty snow littered the streets under a grey and damp Toronto sky. Al's old plain bag flopped at her side. Her feet crunched over frozen slush. She still hadn't decided what to do about the new knapsacks.

Use them both, changing every other day so it wouldn't seem she was picking a favourite? But that would be dumb, a nuisance.

Just use the one from her dad because using the one from her mom would hurt his feelings and way out in Alberta she wouldn't know the difference anyway?

Except she sort of wanted to use the one from her mom. It would be rotten to just leave it in a lump in her closet.

A hand-made bag like that couldn't have been cheap. It was a big deal for her mother to put out money like that.

But the look on her dad's face — how could she even begin to think it was worth it?

Al kicked a chunk of ice, sent it skittering along the sidewalk. Why did choosing between a couple of stupid Christmas presents have to be so complicated?

Over the holiday something had happened to Pickles' hair.

"She must have had a bad dye job or something," one of the girls said.

Someone else giggled. "It has a definite green tinge, doesn't it."

"What do you expect," said one of the boys, "with a name like Pickles?"

"Yeah, it's just taking a while for her to turn into one, right?"

Al smiled. It was a dumb joke, but the image of her teacher turning green by inches, starting at the top, was pretty irresistible.

"We're going to have Book Buddies this morning," Pickles said. It was hard to concentrate on anything but the green fluff bobbing at the top of her head. "Lots of the Grade Ones have new books they're eager to read, or have you read to them."

"Did you bring a book today?" Al asked when she picked up Roberto. He pulled the little book she had given him from his pocket, his big brown eyes looking up at her. It seemed he held her hand a little tighter than usual on the way down the hall to the library.

Someone got to the bathtub before them, so they settled on the sofa. "Are you reading to me today," Al asked, "or am I reading to you?"

Roberto poked her arm.

"I'm reading to you?"

He nodded.

She began the story, and turned the page. "Do you want to take a turn? You know all the words in this book."

He shook his head.

She continued to read. Roberto snuggled in closer to her side. Right through to the end of the book, he had no questions, no comments. He didn't point out anything in the pictures either. Al closed the book, but still he kept leaning against her.

"Do you feel okay?"

She felt him shrug.

"Are you sick?"

He shook his head.

"How about you teach me some new Spanish? Can you teach me to say Happy New Year?"

He shook his head again.

"Something's the matter. Can't you tell me?"

Al felt Roberto take a deep breath. Then he sat up, looked at her, and said, "We're getting a divorce."

"Oh, Robbie. Your mom and dad, you mean?"

"Everybody," Roberto said. "My daddy is going away." He was trying so hard to be brave, but his chin wobbled a little.

Al pulled him close to her again. "It'll be okay, it'll be okay."

But it wouldn't be. Not really. He'd probably spend the rest of his life wishing he was with whichever parent he wasn't with, or having a good time with his dad but being careful not to let his mom think he'd had too good a time, and vice versa. He might even get stuck with some dumb court order like she had. Or end up living in two places all the time, like Natalie.

"My dad moved away when I was little, you know, but I still got to see him." She tried to make herself sound cheerful. "Now I'm even living at his house."

"I might live with my daddy. He said."

"Would you like that?"

Roberto shrugged.

"Or would you rather live with your mom?"

With the attitude of a little boy who knows with certainty what he wants but knows also that he can't have it, Roberto slid off the sofa and tucked his book in his pocket. "Both," he said.

Al swallowed. "I know."

twenty seven

By four o'clock the frozen slush had turned to slop. Al stuck her sodden shoes by the heat and changed into dry socks. A pack of new boot laces was on the kitchen counter along with a note:

> *Had to go in to the office for a while. There's stuff in the fridge and cupboard for salad and spaghetti and meatballs. If you could start getting dinner ready, I should be home by six.*
>
> *Love, Dad*

Al squeezed the cold ground beef between her palms. Meatballs were wonderful. Nothing complicated about a meatball. Just squish it, roll it, and dump it in the pan. If a meatball had any feelings, it kept them to itself. And these meatballs were perfect. Perfect spheres, perfectly medium-sized. And not one fell to pieces in the pan.

The water was boiling and the thingy with the different sized holes for measuring the spaghetti made it easy to cook the perfect amount. Her dad had picked it up at the grocery store after the time she cooked enough pasta to feed them for a week. The salad looked perfect, too, in the new bowl Susan had given her dad for Christmas. Nothing like cooking a good meal, unless it was painting one, to take your mind off things like sad Book Buddies and identical knapsacks.

At five to six, Al munched a stick of raw pasta, and dropped the rest into the boiling water. Her timing was going to be perfect. Dinner would be ready the minute her dad walked in. She went to the living room to answer the phone.

"The job took longer than I thought, but I'm leaving now, I'll be about twenty minutes."

While the spaghetti cooked and the sauce simmered, Al went to her room with two green garbage bags. With her eyes closed, she put a knapsack in each. She tied knots in the tops, cleared floor space in the middle of the room, and swirled the slippery plastic bags in circles to mix them up. She juggled them in the air for a minute and let them drop.

"Eenie meenie miney mo." She had decided she would use the one at the end of the chant for school. The other she would keep as an overnight bag. "If he hollers let him go, Eenie meenie miney mo."

Okay. Leaving the loser in its plastic bag, Al stuck it in the closet. Her fingers fumbled with the knot in the other bag. She pulled out the denim and tapestry knapsack that would be for every-day, held it up, and turned it over. Which? . . .

Yes! If she couldn't tell if this was the knapsack from her dad or her mom, no one else would be able to either.

"I'm home! Al?"

The spaghetti was puffed up big as hoses, the sauce burnt on the bottom, the salad wilted. "I guess I shouldn't have left it."

"It's not your fault. I should have known this meeting might run late."

"What happened?"

Al's dad poked the bloated pasta with a fork. "If we went out to eat, would you feel bad all your hard work was wasted?"

"Can we go to that place with the menus as big as the

tables?"

After they ordered — they both decided they still felt like spaghetti — Al said, "You never told me what happened at work."

"Oh, nothing important. We were just trying to figure out a way to avoid some potentially bad publicity over a proposed condo project. Remember those old buildings they're tearing down?"

Al munched on a breadstick. "I forget."

"Well, the people who wanted the landlord to fix the places up are hopping mad that he sold them to us instead. They're threatening to move into our lobby." He took a sip from his drink. "They claim there's nowhere else in the city they can afford to live."

Al thought of people she'd been making muffins for since Christmas, the woman with the red fedora, and the family in the alley she never saw again. "They're right, aren't they?"

Her dad reached for a breadstick. "What did you do at school today?"

Al shrugged. "Nothing much."

twenty eight

M s. Pickles scribbled some phrases on the board. "Does anyone know the origin of any of these expressions?"

"Achilles heel," Gregory said, and retold the whole Greek myth to explain it. He also knew all the rules of billiards and how 'behind the eight ball' had come to mean in a very difficult position.

"Very good, Gregory." Ms. Pickles' green topknot quivered. She pointed to the next expression on the board. "Does anyone know where 'the wisdom of Solomon' comes from?"

No hands went up, not even Gregory's.

"Long ago," Ms. Pickles launched into the story, "two mothers were fighting over a baby. Both mothers claimed the baby was hers. They argued and argued, but were unable to settle the dispute. So they went to King Solomon. They agreed he was a wise king and would be able to determine, once and for all, whose baby this was."

A few heads bobbed in recognition. One of the kids said, "This sounds familiar. Not 'the wisdom of Solomon' though."

"I think he had some way of telling whose kid it was 'cause he was so smart, or something."

"Like DNA," someone piped up, "only different, because this was olden times, right?"

"Does anyone know how King Solomon determined

which woman was the mother of the baby?"

A girl in the back of the class spoke up. "I know. The king said, 'Bring me a sword', and they did. Then he said, 'Cut the kid in two, and give half the kid to one mother and half to the other mother'. The first mother said, 'Okay, that sounds fair'. And the second mother said, 'No, please don't cut the child in two. Let her keep the child'. Something like that?"

"That's very good, Kris," Ms. Pickles said.

"I don't get it."

"Can you finish the story, Kris?"

"I forget the rest."

Al raised a cautious finger. "King Solomon gave the baby to the second mother."

"Because . . . "

"He knew the second one had to be the baby's true mother, and not the first one," Al explained, "because no real mother would agree to letting her baby get cut in half."

"Hey," enthused Gregory, "that was one smart king."

Ms. Pickles nodded. "'The wisdom of Solomon'."

february

twenty nine

February 14
Dear Sam,

> *Is we friends or is we ain't?*
> *Tell me quick, before I faint.*

> *Happy Valentine's Day.*

> *How are you? I haven't got a letter from you in ages.*

> *According to those antique pamphlets they gave out in Health last year, I'm "a young woman now". Thank goodness Susan was here when it happened. I'd have died if I had to ask my dad to buy pads.*

> *Picture this, okay? — I'm tied up in this courtroom while this judge listens to my mom and dad arguing about who should have custody and everything. After they finish, the judge says, "No problem. Cut the kid in two." I'm waiting to see which one of them says, "Oh, no, we can't have that, you take her." Only instead they say, both at the same time, "Great idea!" Of all the times for my parents to agree!*

> *This didn't really happen. Just in a nightmare I had after Pickles made us talk about this dumb story at school.*

> *Your friend till the comic strips, Al*

thirty

Al's eyes almost crossed trying to focus on Susan's fingers as they steered the scissors along the shaggy ends of her brown bangs. She refocused on her reflection in the bathroom mirror. Good. Susan wasn't cutting them too short. She hated it if her eyebrows showed.

"There you go. You should be able to see for another month or so now."

"Thanks." Al held her long hair up off her neck. It was . . . interesting, without hair hanging beside her face. She looked different. Older? "Susan, I've been thinking . . . What do you think?"

"Of what? Having it cut?"

She let it fall again down her back. "Maybe not."

Susan wound Al's hair in a thick knot at the base of her neck. "It's lovely hair."

"Except for trims, I haven't had it cut since Grade One."

"You won't make the decision lightly then, will you? Maybe you'll want to talk it over with your mom."

"Maybe." Al tried to look at the side of her face in the mirror. "If I do decide to get it cut, will you do it?"

"I think if you decide to get it cut — if you do — you'll want a real hairdresser. I like Yvonne over at Cut & Curl on Mount Pleasant. I could make an appointment for you — if you're sure you want to do it."

"I don't know yet."

The phone rang and Susan let the long hair tumble.

"Thanks." Al ran to answer it.

"Mom. Hi."

"Hi, Allie. How's my favourite valentine?"

"Good. How's mine?"

"Not too bad."

"Something happened, Mom."

"Something?"

"My period. I got it."

"Well! Well, I guess I shouldn't be surprised, should I?"

"I am almost thirteen, Mom. Lots of girls start a lot younger than me."

"Yes, of course. Well, you may not be a little girl any more, but you'll always be my little girl."

"Mo-om."

"Never mind Mo-om. It's true."

"I know. Just like you'll always be my Big Momma."

thirty one

Every day for a week, every time she looked in the mirror, having her hair cut felt more and more the right thing to do.

Mom, she imagined herself saying, *I'm thinking of getting my hair cut.*

Oh, Sweetie, but you've had long hair since you were in Kindergarten. Are you sure? You won't be able to wear it in braids any more. It's a big step, Allie, why don't you wait till you come home and I can help you decide. But it didn't matter, really, what her mom would say. And she didn't need Susan to make an appointment for her either.

Al looked up Cut & Curl in the phonebook and called for an appointment with Yvonne. Saturday at two.

She woke early Saturday morning and couldn't go back to sleep. Her dad got up an hour later to the smell of baking muffins.

"Goodness." He reached for a warm one on the rack. "You're not still making muffins for strangers, are you?" Steam poured out when he broke his open.

"Yes, Dad. I am. And I buy the stuff out of my allowance, so it's nothing for you to get in a huff about."

He shook his head. "Just be careful, alright?"

"I am."

Later, when the muffins were cool, she tucked most of them in little bags and stuck them in the freezer. She put a couple in her patchwork knapsack for her trek over to

Mount Pleasant.

Puddles of snow dotted the edges of lawns and curbs. It was so mild, Al walked with her jacket open. What would it feel like to not have her hair flopping heavy against her back? What would her dad say when she got back home? What would her mom say? Was she really going through with this, or would she chicken out at the last minute?

"So," Yvonne said at ten past two. "A few inches off the bottom just to tidy things up?" Al's wet hair hung straight down her back. Behind her in the mirror stood the blonde hairdresser with black eyebrows, comb in one hand, scissors in the other.

Al stared straight ahead and with unexpected calm said, "No, I'd like it short." She scissored her fingers around a clump of hair just above her shoulder. "To about here."

"Oh, my," Yvonne said. "That must be about a lifetime of hair, eh?" She crossed her arms across her ample chest. "You've thought about this real careful, have you?"

Al nodded.

"Your mom will be wanting it kept though, eh? I know I sure would if my daughter ever got hers chopped. Shall we braid it so you can take it home?"

"My mom doesn't actually — " The worried look on Yvonne's face stopped her. "Yes, that would be a good idea."

Yvonne wound an elastic around Al's hair between her shoulders.

Al said, "I think she still has my baby hair in a little envelope."

"I can imagine." Yvonne separated the ponytail into three strands and began to braid them. "What I wouldn't give for nice thick hair like this." She wrapped another elastic at the end of the braid. "You're sure about this, now?" The scissors beside her head caught sunlight from the window. "Can't change your mind after, you know. It's speak now or forever hold your peace."

Al smiled. "I know." But when the shears came closer to

her head she shut her eyes.

It wasn't over in a second the way she'd imagined. At the sound of metal slicing through the thick cord of hair, she winced. Till finally the scissors closed with a resounding "Click." Her hair sprang free.

Yvonne handed her the amputated braid, thick and spongey in her fist. Al swallowed. "Could you put it in a bag?" She focused then on the girl in the mirror, who somehow took over answering Yvonne's questions: *Would you like it layered or blunt? Bangs straight across or tapered down?*

Snip. Snip. Snip. Al watched herself become new.

Her head felt so light she almost flew home. The unseasonably warm breeze lifted her hair off her ears. She twisted her neck back and forth and laughed at the feel of silk slapping against her face.

For fun, instead of just walking in and saying *What do you think, Dad?*, Al stopped on the porch and rang the bell.

"I'm afraid we don't need . . . Alison! Honey, come in! Why, it's lovely! Whatever made you? . . . " He laughed. "I didn't even recognize you."

"I wonder what Mom will think of it."

He turned her in circles. "What about you?" he asked. "Do you like it?"

Al ran her hands through the crisp ends. "I do. I love it."

"Well, that's the most important thing." He shook his head. "My little girl. Where did she go?"

Al poked his soft gut. "That's supposed to be Mom's question, Dad, not yours."

thirty two

The snow was so deep you couldn't tell where the sidewalks were, or the curbs at the sides of the roads. It blew in drifts that turned steps, bushes, and parked cars into a swooping series of snow sculptures. And still it continued to fall in swirling, endless clouds.

"Hi, Kim?" Al twisted the phone cord around her finger. "I guess we're not going to get to that movie this aft, eh?"

"I don't think anybody's going much of anywhere. My mom won't let me anyway."

"Yeah, my mom would be the same. So, well, another time."

"Wouldn't it be something if they had to shut down school on Monday?"

"They'll have plowed by then, won't they?"

"Yeah, probably. What a waste, to have a good storm like this on a Saturday."

"Yeah. Well, see you."

Al flipped through the TV guide that came with the paper. It usually arrived between the doors before she got up, but with the storm it hadn't been delivered till almost noon.

There was nothing on TV. And she'd read both her magazines already. She wandered into her room and took out a sketchpad. She did a little drawing of her old clay cat. She thought about calling her mom to see if it was snowing in Alberta, but it would be a lot cheaper tomorrow. Not that her dad seemed to think much about wasting money, but it was a hard habit to break after all those years.

Al shuffled her slippered feet out to the kitchen and stared into the cupboard, looking for inspiration. But the canned beans and instant soups didn't do it. Chips would have been good. It was a chip kind of day, chips with dip. But there weren't any chips.

Outside the front window the snow blew into sharp peaks and continued to fall. Al loved big winter storms in Alberta. Like the blizzard that hit overnight when she and her mom were at Aunt Karen's cabin one weekend. They'd headed up during a chinook. No one had forecast the drastic change. So there they were inside the muffled little cabin, figuring out how to make their food last if they couldn't get out for a few days, feeding the fire, and telling storm stories. Before the end of the morning some snowmobilers saw the smoke from their chimney, hauled them out to the road, and helped them unbury their car. Al sighed.

"That was a big one," her dad said, looking up from the newspaper. "Penny for your thoughts?"

"I don't know. Just . . . I don't know."

"If you're looking for something to do, you could come down to the darkroom with me. I've got some old film I haven't found time to develop. I thought I'd do it today."

Al followed her dad downstairs and watched him set up his equipment. Trays, bottles, paper. "Okay," he said, "you flick that switch now."

Only an amber light glowed in the corner. "Gees," Al said, "how do you see to do anything?"

"It's not called a darkroom for nothing, you know."

Gradually Al's eyes adjusted and found the trays of liquid her dad had prepared. She stared at the paper as it floated to the bottom of the tray. Smudges began to appear. Faint ones. Or did they? Was she so keen to see something happen that she imagined them? No. One of the blurry blotches was coming into focus.

It was her face framed by an unruly mop of hair. Without

thinking she raised her hand to the clean edge of her almost-new haircut.

With a pair of tongs, her dad lifted the dripping print — she was in her room, beside her bed the first day she saw it. He lowered it into the other tray of liquid. "You have to do this to set it," he explained.

But nothing was ever really set, was it? Like, the girl in the watery image was her. Of course, it was. But so young. Had she really changed that much since coming here? That girl below the liquid surface was the last "Alison" her mom had seen.

In the next picture she was on her bike, and there was Natalie, the day they met and rode down the Don Valley. She'd hadn't seen much of her since then, because of how her days with her parents worked out. Too bad.

They worked through more prints — of the picnic, of Christmas Eve, and Christmas itself. The reflection of the almost-teenager gazing up at her from the pool of developing fluid was so different from the one under the water with her childish, style-less straggle. But there were other changes, too. More subtle ones. Like her posture. She was closed somehow in August. As if she felt temporary in her body.

Maybe it wasn't her body she'd felt temporary about, though that showed signs of change too since last summer. Maybe it was in her dad's house she'd felt temporary, perched till the court order would let her go home. Home.

"Is it hot in here?" A trickle of sweat tickled down her side.

"It's warm," her dad answered. "You have to keep the chemicals a certain temperature." He placed a hand on Al's elbow. "Are you okay?"

She nodded. But tears stung in the back of her throat. Because — but this was just too weird — she was feeling pretty at home where she was.

From upstairs came a muffled tap. "Dad, is that the

door?"

"Why don't you go see? I'm at a point it's okay to stop if it's someone for me."

Al squinted in the bright light and took the stairs two at a time.

"Kim!"

"What's wrong with your eyes? Have you been crying?"

"I was in the darkroom with my dad. How'd you get over here?"

"My mom said if I shovelled us out, I could come over. I thought we might go toboganning." Kim leaned her toboggan against the brick wall beside the door. "But do you mind if I come in and warm up a bit first?" She stamped the snow off her boots.

Al's dad poked his nose around the corner. "It's for you, is it?"

"Yeah. It's my friend from school. Kim."

"Hello, Kim. Nice to meet you at last."

"You too."

Al dragged Kim off to her room. She chucked pillows down off her bed and they lounged on the floor.

"Your dad seems nice."

"Yeah. You'd like my mom, too. I go back to live with her this summer."

"Where?"

"Alberta."

"Wow. Do you do that every summer?"

"No, I actually live with my mom. I'm just with my dad this year 'cause of a dumb court order."

Kim sat up straight. "I don't want you to move to Alberta. We just got to be friends. You can't move away."

"So, do you live with both your parents, or what?"

It took Kim a minute before she said, "Just with my mom." She tacked on quietly, "Sort of." She stroked Flash's fur as he strutted by.

"Sort of?"

"She's got this friend."

"So does he live with you — your mom's friend?"

"She. Yeah." Kim nodded toward Al's bulletin board above her desk. "So, who's the cat in that picture?"

"That's my mom's cat, Rumplestiltskin."

"Who's the girl?"

"My best friend. Well, she was my best friend. I mean she sort of still is, but it's kind of weird."

"It must be hard to have a best friend who lives thousands of miles away."

"We write letters, but it's not like being together." Al pulled Flash against her chest. "It's not just that though. Sam's never met my dad, but she always seems to think he's some kind of villain . . . 'Cause of the custody battle and stuff. And 'cause she's heard my mom complain about him not sending enough child support. Stuff like that. She never seems to get it that I love both my parents, even if they can't stand each other. You know?"

Kim frowned. "I think so. I never knew my dad, but it's sort of separate, parents' stuff and your stuff. Is that what you mean?"

"Yeah." Flash squirmed out of Al's arms. "Sam and I promised when I left we'd be best friends forever. But . . . I don't know."

"Stuff changes."

"I hope you don't think I'm getting mushy on you or anything, but . . . " Al twisted a short strand of hair around her finger. "It sort of feels like you're my best friend now."

"And that's not supposed to be mushy?" Kim laughed and threw a pillow at Al's head. "Shut up, will you? And let's go tobogganing."

march

thirty three

From among the buzz of students leaving the school, Al caught the accented voice of a woman in the office. "Roberto," the woman said. "Roberto Salvatore. I come to take my son home from school." Al turned. Her Book Buddy's mother was a haggard-looking woman with dark circles under her eyes.

"I'm sorry," the school secretary said. "Roberto's father came to take him for his dentist appointment just after lunch."

"No!" Roberto's mother cried out loud. "There is no dentist." Al grabbed Kim's coat sleeve, her stomach sinking. A knot of students started to form in the hallway outside the office. "My baby!" Roberto's mother wailed. "Please, you call police."

A teacher ushered the ogling students along the hall to the outside door. The secretary led Mrs. Salvatore into the principal's office, one arm around her shaking shoulders.

Before classes started the next morning, the news was all over the school. When Roberto's mother came looking for him yesterday, his father already had him on a plane to wherever it was he came from. Some kids said South America. Others said somewhere in Europe.

"Poor kid." Al mindlessly pulled books from her locker. "He must be so scared."

"At least it's not like he got kidnapped by a stranger who might hurt him or anything," Kim said.

"But what's he going to think is going on?"

"I saw a movie on TV once where the dad abducting a kid told him his mother was dead."

Al slammed shut her locker. "There should be a law."

"Against kidnapping? There is."

"There should be a law that says people can't have kids unless they promise to stay together and take care of them properly till they're grown up."

"I never had a dad. I'm okay." Kim and Al headed into homeroom. "Besides, isn't that what getting married is supposed to be? From this day forward, till death do us part, and all that?"

"Yeah, so how come I'm caught in my stupid custody thing and Roberto is — who knows where?" Al plunked her books on her desk. "There must be something better."

Kim chewed on the corner of her bottom lip, then looked away.

"What?" Al asked. "What were you going to say?"

"Isn't this weekend your birthday?"

"Okay, so don't tell me. I don't care."

Kim sat down beside her. "So, what are you doing for your birthday?"

"I don't know." Al dug into her knapsack for a pen. "At least I don't have to worry that my parents are going to both give me the same thing like they did at Christmas."

"How do you know?"

"My mom already sent me hair clips."

"Oops."

"I know. I can't believe I forgot to tell her."

"Forgot? There's no way you forgot to tell her something that big."

Ms. Pickles stood in front of the class, eyeballing students who hadn't settled yet. Kim whispered, "Why didn't you tell her?"

"I don't know. She'll feel bad 'cause she wasn't there. And 'cause I didn't ask her first."

"So, whose hair is it?"

"I know, I'll tell her sometime. Or send her a picture or something."

thirty four

A l climbed down the ladder and stumbled across her
bedroom. Stuck on the door was a new poster:

DANGER ZONE!
TEENAGER WITHIN!!

"Happy Birthday, Alison." Her dad came in with juice
and a muffin, a candle stuck in its top. "You'll have a real
cake later, of course," he said. "Do you like your poster?"

Al smiled and blew out the flame. "Thanks, Dad."

"Come on down when you've finished," he said. "I have
to get back to something in the kitchen."

Was he baking her a cake? Her mom had made one for
all her other birthdays, a double fudge layer cake, big
enough for all her friends to have a piece after the waterslide
party. With her juice, Al washed down a twinge of homesick, got dressed, and wandered down to see what her dad
was up to in the kitchen.

"Surprise!"

"Kim! I didn't know you were going to be here!"

"Happy Birthday." Kim smiled and pushed a present
across the table.

Al opened it — a box of chalk pastels. "Thanks!" Susan
arrived soon after and gave her bath stuff. "I wasn't sure
about the scent," she said, "but Natalie assured me it was
what you'd want." Then Ryan and his parents from across
the street dropped in to say happy birthday. Susan helped

Al's dad set out the buffet brunch — croissants and jams, yogurt and fresh fruit.

"Dad, I thought we were going out for dinner tonight."

"We are."

"Dinner and a party?"

"Sure, and in between we can go see that movie you've been wanting to see. There have been too many birthdays when I couldn't do what I wanted for you." Her dad gave her a shoulder hug. "Just don't expect the same treatment next year."

The sudden silence made his words bigger and louder. His face reddened and he mumbled, "If you're still here . . . I know it's difficult."

Everyone looked at Al, but she didn't have an answer. How could she, in front of all these people? She was about to charge from the room when Susan said, "Well, a person only celebrates becoming a teenager once in a lifetime. It's only right to make a big occasion of it. Right?"

"Hear, hear!" Kim said.

"I'll drink to that." Ryan's dad poured himself another cup of coffee.

Ryan dragged Al to the sofa with a book. She looked at it with him, but out of the corner of her eye watched Susan in her purple velour track suit, encouraging people to help themselves to brunch. How was it some people knew exactly what to say to make everything okay, when a minute before, it wasn't? No wonder her dad liked her. The phone rang and Al picked it up.

"Happy Birthday, Teenager. Did my present arrive on time?"

Al pressed the phone to her ear and covered the other with her hand. "Yeah, thanks, Mom . . . Yeah, they're really nice . . . No I haven't had a chance yet."

"When you do, get your dad to take a picture, okay?"

"Yeah."

"Are you having a good birthday?"

"It's alright. But there's no waterslide party or anything. And I wish I could see you."

"Well, you'll be home for your next birthday, eh?"

"I've gotta go now, Mom. There's people here and stuff."

thirty five

Dinner out was just her and her dad. She got dressed up, wore a skirt even. Black with a pinstripe, like her dad's jacket. He'd given her money to buy it last month when she complained her old skirt was too snug around the hips.

The hostess seated them at a table overlooking the street. It was raining outside and traffic hissed by slowly. The slick black road glistened with neon reflections.

"It was raining the day you were born, too," Al's dad said after they ordered a drink. "I didn't want to go to work that morning, I had a feeling it was going to be the Big Day, but your mom insisted I go, so I did. She called me an hour later. I was so excited I missed the turnoff for the hospital."

"Did Mom get mad?"

"Not too mad."

He swirled the ice cubes in his drink.

"Were you in the delivery room when I was born?"

"I wouldn't have missed your arrival for the world." He smiled. "The doctor let me lift you onto your mom's belly. You were so perfect, Alison."

"Were? You mean I'm not still?" Al dug into the flaming cheese she ordered for an appetizer, then the lamb souvlaki — all the while chatting with her dad about school, art, computers, and the movie they'd seen before dinner. She told him about Roberto, too.

"Would you be shocked if I told you I entertained thoughts of doing that when you were little?"

"Da-ad! Yes!"

"I missed you. I wanted to be able to read you bedtime stories and tuck you in at night, kiss your dirty knees when you came in crying." As if he realized he might be laying it on a bit thick, he lightened up, almost making fun of his own wishes. "I wanted to go to meet-the-creature nights every fall and hear you sing at school concerts every spring."

"You didn't miss much, Dad. Which you would know if you ever heard me sing."

"I have heard you, actually."

"What? When?"

"What's that thing you do in the shower?"

She would have hidden behind her long hair if she still had it. Instead she teased, "Would you like me to sing it for you now?"

"Not just now." Her dad nodded toward a group of waiters and waitresses heading toward their table. A sparkler sputtered and hissed in the middle of the hugest piece of double fudge chocolate layer cake Al had ever seen. All the staff and her dad sang Happy Birthday. Even people at nearby tables joined in.

Al licked chocolate icing from her finger. "Did you know this was my favourite?"

"I know lots of things about you, Alison." The wrinkles at the corners of his eyes showed it wasn't all happy, what he knew.

The waitress brought them forks and together they demolished the cake.

"Well," her dad said, "we've been here for a long time and the waitress hasn't had to bring you crayons."

"Hardly."

"Guess that means you're pretty well grown up, eh?"

Al laughed. "Not exactly."

Her dad reached into the pocket of his jacket. On the

white tablecloth between them he placed a tiny velvet box. Al looked at the box, then at him. "You already gave me a present."

"This isn't really a present. It's something that belonged to my mother and to my grandmother before that." He pushed the box a little closer. "Open it."

Al lifted the hinged lid. Inside the box was a ring. Tiny white stones were set around a slightly larger blue stone. "Since I never had sisters," her dad explained, "your grandmother said I should hold on to it till you were old enough to take care of it."

"I wish I could remember her."

"She died before you were even two, but boy, did she think you were the cat's snowsuit." He removed the ring from the box and slipped it onto Al's finger. "It's almost a hundred years old, this ring."

Al turned her hand to catch the light in the stones. "Wow."

thirty six

March 10

Dear Al,

Happy Birthday!

I bet you thought I'd forget, didn't you? But how could I forget the birthday of the best friend I've had since Grade One? How does it feel to be a really and truly teenager? What are you doing for it?

I hope you'll be back for my birthday in July. I've been working on my mom to let me have a mixed party this year. But actually as long as you're here I won't care if the boys can come. By the way, Jason is now going out with Charlene Maguire. Gag me with a spoon. It's a wonder her eyelashes don't fall out the way she bats them around these days.

Have an extra piece of cake for me, 'kay?

Your friend, Sam

april

thirty seven

Crocuses and hyacinths popped through the earth. For three days kids showed up at school in shirtsleeves, but the weekend came rainy and cool.

Al lay on her bed, curled round her crampy gut. She reached for a blanket. If her mom was here, she'd wrap the blanket around her. She'd pull her on her lap and rock her. Poor little Allie, she'd say, like she did when Al was little and had growing pains in her legs.

But her mom wasn't here. And she wasn't about to let her dad know why she was feeling lousy. She got off the bed and tried a couple of stretches the gym teacher said could help ease cramps. They didn't really, but it was better than doing nothing.

Downstairs she said, "I'm going to light a fire, 'kay?"

"Sure. I'll go get us a video."

When he got back, the room was cozy and warm.

"Feel like popcorn?" he asked.

"Why?" Al said, beating him to the punch line. "Do I look like popcorn?"

While her dad banged around in the kitchen cupboards looking for the popper, she stretched out in front of the fire. In the bottom shelf of the wall unit was a big brown book she hadn't noticed before. She ran her finger through the layer of dust on its cover, blew off the rest, and opened it. A photo album.

And there she was as a baby, with very young-looking

parents. "Look at this, Dad," she called.

She pointed in the photo to a darker, longer-haired version of the man beside her. "You look so young."

"You're looking pretty young yourself." In one of the pictures a pudgy-armed baby smiled up from her swing. "That was in our apartment in Calgary."

Al turned the page.

"That's after we moved to Toronto, in the apartment we had here."

"I never knew I lived in Toronto before."

"For a while." He stood abruptly. "I better do the popcorn."

Al flipped through pages and pages of baby pictures before she came to her first Christmas. The woman holding her while she played peek-a-boo with her grampa must be the grandmother she couldn't remember. Al held the page close to her face, searching for a resemblance, and found it — that same crooked tooth she shared with her dad.

And, on her grandmother's hand — was it? Yes. Al held the ring on her own finger to her lips.

Then her first birthday. She laughed at her fat cheeks and punk hair. Lots more pages of pictures — in parks, at petting farms — Alison walking, Alison eating, Alison laughing, Alison sleeping. Then the birthday cake had two candles on it.

On the next page, it was Christmas at her grampa's in Calgary, and she was older. Much older than two. Five maybe. Al flipped back. She must have missed something, or turned two pages by mistake. At least.

But no. On one page she was a chubby little toddler, on the next — suddenly — quite a lean little girl. She might even have been six. After that there were pictures from each Christmas in Alberta and each summer in Toronto. They ended the Christmas before last.

After all those everyday baby pages, it seemed awful how it was suddenly just opening presents at her grampa's and riding the train at Centre Island, or other summer-in-Toronto stuff. There were no pictures of her first day of school, her big bright paintings stuck on the fridge, or the cast she got when she fell out of the tree down by the river and broke her leg. Because, of course, her dad wasn't around then to take them.

But she knew it had been like that. There was something else here that wasn't right.

The popcorn machine whirred loudly in the kitchen. Al flipped back to where she jumped from being two to being five. It was like there were pictures missing. But all the spaces in the album were full. The popcorn began to explode.

"Dad," — he came into the living room with a heaping bowl — "how come there's no pictures of me for a few years? It's like I go suddenly from being a baby to being a little girl."

"You know your mother and I split up when you were only two. I didn't see you as much after that."

"I know, but for a long time you don't even have pictures of me at Christmas or in the summer."

Her dad placed the bowl of popcorn on the coffee table like it was precious crystal full of delicate eggs. "That's because I didn't see you."

She wanted to jump up, start the video, and stuff her mouth full of buttery popcorn, forget she'd ever discovered this album. But she couldn't. She couldn't move. Her dad, too, was sitting very still. A log in the fireplace collapsed.

"Why?"

"Your mother . . . " He got up and threw another log in the fire. He poked at the dying embers till they caught. "Let's just say it was hard for me to see you."

"Because Mom moved back to Alberta?"

"Is that what she's told you?"

"I just thought it."

"Well, it wasn't just that." He sighed. Like he was mad

but didn't want to show it. Al thought he was going to explain, but all he said was, "It was very difficult. Shall I start this movie?"

What was that supposed to mean? It was very difficult. Flames cracked in the fireplace.

Only one thing. After they split up, her mom wouldn't let him come and see her.

"Not for me." Al headed for the stairs.

"Do you want any of this popcorn?"

"No."

"Please don't be angry, Alison. I wanted to see you."

"I know."

She lay on her bed, staring at the ceiling, as tears trickled into her ears. That was why he started the custody fight. She wouldn't let him see her. What else was he supposed to do? Flash jumped to the windowsill, and onto Al's stomach. He kneaded her chest with his paws, purring loudly. It hurt, but it didn't matter.

thirty eight

April 20

Dear Sam,

*I have found out the awfullest thing. I don't know
what to do. I know you will have trouble believing this,
but it isn't my dad's fault about the custody fight and
me being here this year. It's my mom's. I can't come back
there and live with her. I don't even want to talk to her
on the phone.*

*She wouldn't let him see me, Sam. But I'm his
daughter too. I don't know if I would have even seen
him at Christmas and in the summers if it wasn't for
that court order. My parents lived in Toronto when I
was a baby and when they split up my mom took me
back to Alberta and wouldn't let my dad see me.*

I saw some pictures yesterday and figured it out.

Your friend till the banana splits, Al

thirty nine

Hello?"
"Sweetie, I haven't heard from you in a while. I must have missed your call last Sunday."
Maybe 'cause I didn't call you. "Yeah."
"Is everything okay?"
Fine, sure, just fine, you always made Dad sound like some stingy creep, but you wouldn't even let him see me when I was little. "Just busy."
"Guess Art Camp's coming up soon, eh?"
"In June."
"Is the weather getting better there yet?"
"Yup."
"What about your Book Buddy? Did they ever find him?"
"Yup."
"It's awful, isn't it, the things some people will do after a divorce."
"Yeah, I gotta go."

may

forty

The rumpled old shoe didn't look rumpled enough. It was too flat on the page.

Al pressed the dark chalk into her drawing. What she included in her portfolio didn't decide whether or not she could go to Art Camp, just which artist she'd work with. But she did want to submit the best samples of her work she could. And it was amazing how a bit of black emphasizing the folds, and white to bring forward where the light hit, could make a thing look more three-dimensional.

She flipped through a few more of her drawings and paintings. What else to include? She looked at her watch. Time to go meet her dad at work. She tucked the rejects and "undecideds" into the back of her closet. Her foot bumped against the tin of cornflower blue paint.

With a few muffins in her knapsack and a bus ticket in her pocket, she hurried over to Yonge Street. It was a windy spring day that felt more like fall, raw and damp. She handed her regular at the top of the subway stairs a muffin. "What kind today?" he asked.

"Date bran."

"My favourite."

"You say that whatever kind I bring." Al bounced down the stairs.

As the subway car rattled through the tunnel, rocking from side to side, she stared above the seat at the ad for pink french fries — at least that's what it looked like. Beside the doors sat a man wearing a brown plaid jacket who looked kind of like a boy in the special class at her old school. What was his name? Lennie.

He had a flattish face and his tongue looked almost too big for his mouth. Could he read, Al wondered? How did he manage the TTC by himself if he couldn't?

The train stopped and someone who looked like the brother in love with his sister on Al's soap opera got on. He was tall, his black jeans were skin tight, and his jacket had a kazillion zippers.

Zippers spotted the person Al could only think of as Big Lennie and yelled, "Hi, buddy, good to see ya. How are ya, man?"

Big Lennie smiled, Zippers went over and punched him on the shoulder the way guys do, and Big Lennie kept smiling.

At her old school a lot of people who were supposed to be pretty cool were actually quite mean to kids in the special class. Teachers were always having to stop their teasing — their bullying, really. It was neat these two guys could be friends.

Then Zippers said, "You're in my seat, buddy." He started pulling on the brown plaid jacket. "Out of my seat." Big Lennie looked scared. Al looked around at the other people in the car. Somebody had to say something. But everyone either had their nose in a newspaper or was studiously examining the ads above the seats as if the meaning of life would soon be revealed there. "Move. Now."

The retarded man started to whimper. "No-o." He held onto the bar beside his seat. *Move, Lennie. Why don't you just move!?* But he didn't. He kept hanging on, even though he was almost crying, and the bully kept pulling on his jacket.

Al stood up. She didn't even realize she had till she heard herself speak. "Can't you see that seat is taken?"

Zippers turned slowly, ran his eyes up and down Al's body. "You talking to me?" Blood rushed to her head, making her dizzy. Dead silence. Except the clatter of wheels against the tracks. Everyone was staring. "Yes. I am."

Someone down the car said, "You let go of that man and find somewhere else to sit."

The bully smirked, but seemed at a loss for something to say. As if the plaid jacket had sprouted slimy mould, he let go. The doors opened and he strutted off the train just as cocky and sure as he'd walked on.

"You okay?" asked the man who'd spoken up. "You gotta be careful."

Al nodded. Her grip on the pole loosened. She lowered herself to her seat.

Everyone went back to reading their papers and ads. The train rocked through the dark tunnel.

Big Lennie got up and stood at the door beside Al's seat. He stared straight ahead into the black space between the jostling car and the walls of the tunnel. As the train slowed down, Al checked the station name on the wall. One more stop.

The doors opened and Big Lennie looked down at her. "Thank you, lady," he said. Then he trudged out onto the platform and disappeared.

forty one

Crowds jammed the sidewalk near her dad's office. Al started to elbow her way through. This wasn't the usual crunch of commuters heading for subway stations and parking lots. Some of the people carried placards. Some were shouting.

An earnest-looking man in a suit thrust a microphone in her face. "Tell me. What's your view of Metroplan's plan to demolish blocks of affordable housing in order to build luxury condominiums?"

"I don't think it's fair to build more homes for rich people when there already aren't enough for all the poor people. Especially if you have to tear down poor people's homes to do it."

"As a resident of one of the threatened buildings," the man with the mike said, "how will you be affected by Metroplan's development?"

"Oh, I don't live in one of the buildings."

"How, then, did you come to be involved in this demonstration?"

"My dad works at Metroplan." Before she could explain she wasn't actually part of the demonstration, she was just meeting her dad here 'cause they were going to the Art Gallery after, the man turned and shoved his microphone at someone else.

Al stepped off the elevator on the eighth floor. "Your father is in a meeting," the receptionist told her. "You might as well wait here." Phones rang and faxes rolled out of machines. What if she ended up on the news? Should she explain to her dad what happened, just in case? She flipped through a *Maclean's*, but couldn't pay attention to the words.

Finally her dad came out of his office. "Come on. We better go this way." He took her out through a back door into an alley. They crunched through it to a street where there was no sign of picketers or media people. He walked fast. She almost had to run to keep up.

"Do you want to do this another time, Dad?"

"No, let's just get it over with."

Get it over with? This was supposed to be nice. They were supposed to browse through the new sculpture exhibit, quiet, relaxed. Not tear through it like some nasty chore.

They crossed the street on the yellow light. Al practically tripped up the curb. Her dad's trench coat, which he hadn't bothered to button, flapped ahead of her. Tension lay like a board across his shoulders.

And the sculpture didn't improve his mood. If he couldn't recognize something as an eagle or a woman or something, then to him it was pointless.

They grabbed take-out on the way home. As soon as they got in, he flicked on the TV. "Sorry, Al, but that demonstation today could mean real trouble."

The voice and face of the reporter covering the demonstration sent prickles crawling through Al's whole body. It was like her blood was full of pins. A few faces talked into his dreaded mike, then hers filled the screen. "I don't think it's fair to build more homes for rich people . . . " It was worse than she remembered. "My dad works at Metroplan."

"What the! . . . " Al's dad clicked off the TV. "What did you think you were doing?" In a stupid little kid voice he mimicked her, "*I don't think it's fair.* But it's fair of you to do that!? Do you know I could lose my job over this? I'm supposed to be in charge of public relations on this thing

— and you as good as accuse me, for an audience of thousands, of personally tearing down poor people's houses? After all I have done for you, this is the thanks I get?! You . . . spoiled . . . brat!"

Flash slinked out from under a chair and tore up the stairs.

"All you've done! Like making me come here when all I wanted was to stay home? You buy me everything I want even if I don't want it, as if that can make up for anything." Tears poured down her face, but she kept yelling. "And what am I supposed to do? Be proud of you for putting people out on the street?"

He yelled too, about his job, about her mother. They yelled without listening, about things that had nothing to do with today or even with each other. Everything either of them had ever been mad about, it seemed, was exploding all over the room.

forty two

Al climbed the stairs and searched along the hallway. Her mom wasn't there. She turned along another hall and went down some other stairs, but her mother wasn't there either. She tried to head back to where she'd left her dad, but all the hallways led to more stairs. Up or down, right or left — nowhere led to either of her parents. Finally, at the end of a long straight hall without exits of any kind, she made out a figure. She ran toward it, so relieved to have found someone it didn't matter who it was. She ran, until the details of the figure at the end of the hall became clear. She stopped.

The figure at the end of the hall was herself.

Al rolled over and pulled her covers more snugly around her shoulders. Light from the window shone against her eyelids. She grabbed her alarm. Why hadn't it gone off?

Saturday. You dope. She collapsed into the pillow again.

june

forty three

Hi, Honey, how are you?"

"Fine."

"You didn't call again this week. Are you sure everything's okay?"

"Yeah."

"I miss you, Allie."

"I miss you, too."

"I wanted to tell you, Aunt Karen got the promotion she was after."

"You make it sound like bad news."

"She's moving to the west coast. She's already gone out to find a place."

"Oh. What will you do? You see her all the time."

There was silence on the other end of the line.

"It's okay, Mom. I'll be coming home soon." Even though I don't want to, after what you did.

"You're all I have now, Allie."

But I can't stay with dad now either — after what I did.

"I wish you were coming home today."

"Me too." Lie.

And it was too much. Suddenly she didn't want, any more, to be responsible for anyone else's happiness. She couldn't be.

"Your father will be trying to get you to stay there though, won't he."

"Mom? Why wouldn't you let Dad see me when I was

little?"

"I beg your pardon?"

Al took a deep breath. "Why wouldn't you let Dad — ?"

"I heard you. But he was free to come and see you any time . . . I can't believe this. Did your father tell you? . . . Allie, let me speak to your father."

"But, Mom — "

"I must speak to him. Get him on the phone. Please."

She went to the top of the stairs, cradling the phone against her chest. "Dad! Mom wants to talk to you."

She should hang up now. She knew she should. But she could hear angry voices in the phone. And she needed to. She placed her hand over the mouthpiece and raised the phone to her ear.

"Then why is she accusing me of denying you access? What have you been telling her?"

"Maybe she thinks you moved back west after our split so I wouldn't be able to see her."

"Is that what you told her?"

"I didn't tell her anything." Yes he had. What had he said? "She's mad at me about something else just now. But I can't imagine . . . "

"You knew I had to come back. My family was here. You were my only reason for being in Toronto."

"I know that. But I have never talked about our split with Alison." You did. You said, "I didn't see you for a long time because it was difficult."

"Well, something has changed in the last few weeks. Before that she called me every Sunday. Sometimes we only talked for a few minutes, but she called. I've had to call her at least twice now. And she hasn't talked normally to me in — it must be three weeks."

"Three weeks. That might be around when she found an old photo album here." Heavy sigh. "I can't remember, but she had some questions . . . I wonder . . . "

Silence hummed through the line.

"What kind of questions, John?"

"I think I better go talk to Alison. I'll call you back later."

Al listened for the click of the kitchen phone, then pressed the off button. Heart pounding, she hopped up on her bed with a magazine. She stared at a blur of colour on the page in front of her, as if she didn't know her father was there, standing in the doorway.

"The day we were looking at old photos," he finally said, "I think you misunderstood something."

Al flipped a page with a snap.

"I stopped visiting because seeing you made the times I wasn't seeing you worse — or so I thought — than if I didn't see you at all. I thought I would miss you less if I tried pretending you didn't exist."

The colours in the magazine began to swim.

"It didn't work."

She tried to swallow, but couldn't.

"Your mother never denied me access, Alison. If that's what you thought."

"Oh." Of course she didn't. And thank goodness. She couldn't have stood it to know her mother would pull a stunt like that. Maybe her mom wasn't perfect, but at least she wasn't evil. The world was a good place. And soon she could go home.

"I'm sorry if you misunderstood."

"I guess I should have known she wasn't the bad guy."

"Alison, why does there always have to be a bad guy? When are you going to grow up and quit seeing everything in terms of black and white?"

"I thought caring about other people was grown up. But I guess as soon as what I believe is inconvenient for you and your lousy company, then I'm being childish."

"I thought we were talking about your mother."

"Well, now we're talking about something else. You want me to be grown up, and independent, and think for myself. But only when it suits you. As soon as standing up for what

I believe disagrees with your stupid company — "

"Alison, my stupid company has allowed us to live very comfortably. I haven't noticed you rejecting much of what it's made possible — dinners out, classes at the Art Gallery?"

"No, but — "

"Maybe we both have to learn we can't have things both ways."

"What do you mean?"

"Well, working for Metroplan has its pluses and minuses. And having an outspoken daughter with the guts to stand up for what she believes in — well, it might not always be convenient professionally. But Alison . . . I'm proud of you."

"You are?" Again the colours on the page were swimming.

"I am."

"So, Dad" Al dropped her magazine beside her, "how much does Metroplan give to food banks and homeless shelters and stuff like that?"

"You just don't let go, do you?"

"Aren't you proud of me?"

"Let's just say, I'll look into it, okay?"

forty four

Students and parents filed past the paintings and sculptures displayed around the Art Camp gallery. The whole place was full of beaming faces. Al wished her mom could have been there. "It's okay, Dad, you don't have to like all of it."

The director of the Art Camp spoke into a mike. "We'd like to thank you all for coming to our Open House . . . "

And it was over. Artwork was tucked into cases. Duffel bags and knapsacks were dumped by the gate. Everyone was saying goodbye and exchanging addresses with kids from other schools in the city.

"So, Al, will you really keep in touch?" asked Marika.

"Sure. From somewhere."

Families trickled across the field to their cars. Al placed her nature collage in the trunk. By the time they turned off the dirt road onto the highway, the hot car had cooled off. She babbled on about Marika whose grandparents lived in Medicine Hat, and the other girls in her cabin, the awesome Mr. Sykes who knew so much about shadows and contrast, and the hilarious skits each cabin put on one night. She leaned back against the headrest and sighed. "I can't wait to tell Mom."

They passed fields and farmhouses, small towns, and little lakes, billboards urging travellers to the next McDonalds, the next Comfort Inn. As they got closer to Toronto, they started to see Pick-Your-Own signs. "How about we stop and get some strawberries?" Al's dad suggested.

"You want to pick strawberries?"

"I do it every spring."

She couldn't picture it somehow — her dad squatting in some field with the sun beating down and the sweat pouring off him as he moved along the rows.

"And then what?"

"What do you mean?"

"What do you do with the strawberries? You don't like, make jam or anything."

"Mousse," her dad said. Al swung around trying to see the moose before she realized he meant mousse. "I make flan, too. We can do one for the grad potluck dinner if you'd like."

"As long as it's special enough. 'Cause every year the Grade Sevens do dinner for the Grade Eights, so what gets done this year kind of sets the standard for next year."

"You mean — ?"

"Oh, I don't know what I mean."

forty five

The sailboat skimmed over the water of Lake Ontario. Al lifted her face to the breeze.

"Isn't this just the bluest sky you've ever seen?" Kim said.

"The bluest Toronto sky."

"Oh, you westerners," Kim teased, "always so full of your prairie skies." She tipped her ginger ale can over Al's head, but there was only a drip left.

Kim's mom smiled. She was quiet like her daughter and just as pretty with the same dark hair. Her friend Sally had a laugh that made Al think of wind-chimes. They brought the sail around and landed the boat at the Island. They tried to light the candles on Kim's cake, but the wind kept blowing them out. With the cake in the bottom of the boat, Al and the women sang Happy Birthday. A seagull squawked.

"Make a wish now."

Kim leaned down and blew.

As they pulled away from shore, the roar of a plane coming in to land at the Island Airport drowned out their voices. The sailboat scudded toward the CN Tower, the Skydome, and the other Toronto buildings that stood sharp against the clear sky. Cars crawled like metallic beetles along the Gardiner Expressway.

She knew now what she was going to do. Even though she'd never thought there was anything to decide. The only thing now was: how to break the news?

forty six

It was amazing, Mom. It was like you're not even in the city any more. Except it's right there, and you're just flying across the water."

"It sounds like you had a good time."

"I did."

"Has your father booked your flight yet?"

"Yup. July 12th. Can Sam come to the cabin with us?"

"Sure. Aunt Karen's coming from B.C. for a week, too, but we'll fit everyone in somehow. It'll be fun."

"Mom, I can't wait to see you."

"Me too. It will be so good to have you back where you belong."

Now. "I got Dad to — "

"It's been a long year, hasn't it."

"Mom?"

"Yes?"

. . . the child shall of her own accord determine . . .

"What is it, Allie?"

"You know that paint I told you about? The wall paint, I mean?"

"Cornflower blue, wasn't it?"

"We put it on last weekend."

"You painted . . . " A silence.

"It looks pretty nice. I stencilled a border around the edge of the ceiling. Peace doves. All around the edge. In white. Like the ones you did on that bowl. It looks pretty nice."

"Allie . . . this means . . . "

More waiting.

"Does this mean what I think it means?"

. . . shall of her own accord determine her place of residence.

"Yeah, but I'd come there for Christmas. For sure. And we can talk some more when — "

"Christmas?" Her mother sounded old, confused, tired. In her voice was the hurt, all the hurt Al wanted so badly to avoid.

"Oh, Mom . . . "

forty seven

June 27

Dear Sam,

School is over. Finally.

The second week of July I am flying to Alberta. I'll be there for your birthday. Then I'm going to the cabin with my mom. She said if I want I can invite you for a week. We'll sleep out on the veranda and if we're lucky there'll be a thunderstorm.

Then, guess what.

When I come back to Toronto after the August long weekend, do you want to come, too? I know you think Toronto is a terrible place but I can take you to the Art Gallery and maybe to a baseball game at the Skydome. I hope you can come. Dad says we'll get a cot so you can sleep in my new blue room. (The room is not new, just the blue.)

Have to go now. Kim just came over. She says she would like to meet you, and would you like to go sailing?

Please say yes to everything.

Your friend till Niagara Falls, Al

afterword

Could there really be a court order like the one Alison had to live with? Could a young person really be put in the impossible position of having to choose between parents? Unfortunately, yes. And too many kids know what the courts are capable of in this area. If you or someone you know is having difficulty with any kind of unhappy custody arrangement, there is someone to talk to who cares. Call the Kids Help Phone. 1-800-668-6868.

Is the story Al's dad read to her on the Island a real story? Yes. "Water" by Jean Rand MacEwen appears in *The Blue Jean Collection* published in 1992 by Thistledown Press.

Is there really a book called *The Man Whose Mother Was A Pirate* by Margaret Mahy? Yes! It's a Puffin Book published in 1987 by Orion Books, and it happens to be one of Kathy Stinson's all-time favourite picture books. Check out your bookstore and library and see why Alison and Roberto agreed it's *una buena historia*.

Printed in May 1997 by

VEILLEUX
ON DEMAND PRINTING INC.

in Boucherville, Quebec